YOU'VE GOT TO WANT
TO GO THERE

A TREASURY OF
SHORT STORIES FOR BUSY PEOPLE

You've Got to Want to Go There: A Treasury of Short Stories
for Busy People
Copyright © Charles Miller Hutton 2004

ISBN 1-84426-262-6

First published 2004 by
UPFRONT PUBLISHING LTD
Leicestershire, England

Printed by Lightning Source

You've Got to Want to Go There

A Treasury of
Short Stories for Busy People

CHARLES MILLER HUTTON

UPFRONT PUBLISHING
LEICESTERSHIRE, ENGLAND

This book is dedicated to Janet Hamilton Stocks Hutton,
a woman of considerable perception and courage.

Contents

THE LAST RESORT

It is a little known fact that there is an obscure unwritten clause in the Old Alliance between Scotland and France which permits any born Scot to adopt the motto of any French company, with impunity.

I hereby exercise that right, since the lady in this story, although Scottish, claims direct French descent.

In Paris is the headquarters of one of the largest construction companies in the world, and their motto is 'Nothing great can be accomplished without passion.'

I agree.

Some time ago my wife and I visited one of the most famous and beautiful mountain resorts in the world. We had been there several times on company business and once later privately. We always enjoyed our stay, and the treatment and hospitality.

On our most recent visit we had a particularly attractive room on the fifth floor, overlooking the golf course and the river, all surrounded by snow-capped mountains. Quite perfect, really. The ambience was made all the more perfect when, following a good lunch, we sat at the window enjoying the view and sipping plum brandy.

About a year after this visit I suggested, on impulse, that we should go back for a long weekend. My wife agreed, so I phoned the travel agency and booked two airline tickets to western Canada, a fifteen-hundred-mile flight. I also phoned the hotel, and explained how we had enjoyed previous visits, and particularly the last one.

I requested a room on the fifth or sixth floor, facing east, overlooking the valley, river and golf course. I got a confirmation number and wrote it down after having the reservations clerk repeat the number. All was set for a good weekend, I thought.

In a week or so, we followed the sun to the west and to springtime in snow country. We traveled lightly, easily and relaxed. Until we got to the hotel, that is!

After checking in at the reception desk we were shown to our room on the sixth floor. It was not right, in fact it was all wrong. I didn't like it; my wife didn't like it either. It just would not do, not ever. I suppose the logical thing to have done would have been to pursue the matter right then and see if it could be put right somehow.

However, if I had, in the past, done everything logically, I would not have been able to afford then a hotel of this class, or at least I doubt it.

'Let's forget it for now,' I said to my wife. 'It's just a pity to spoil such a beautiful spring day with a dispute. Why don't we just walk into town, down past the daffodils and snowdrops and look for a place to have a good lunch; I want to think about this problem. I somehow don't know what to do about it.'

My wife immediately replied, 'This is your problem, you solve it; but you're right, let's go for lunch.'

So we did.

We walked casually down the mile or so into town. It was just a beautiful day of bright sunshine, with the towering mountains around the town beyond description. The cool clear, almost icy, air made the prospect of lunch even more inviting.

We had forgotten about our room.

The restaurant was uncrowded, quite intimate, with people serving who were genuinely interested in pleasing their guests.

My wife ordered a bottle of hock and I decided upon a large and very good Scotch. In fact, two. We talked for about fifteen minutes then ordered lunch. My wife had a schnitzel, well prepared and presented. I had a small filet of beef and half a bottle of Bordeaux. All very nice, and soon the glow-worm was alive and well.

In fact, very well, after finishing lunch with a small coffee and Courvoisier – why not, we were on a special weekend!

Unfortunately, I had still not solved the problem of the room yet and time was running out.

I called for a taxi to take us back to the hotel. This was one of my more enlightened ideas that day. The taxi soon arrived, quite an elegant one, not usual for here, really, I thought. In any case, we climbed into the spacious back seat, not without some difficulty, I might add, since my handspun Donegal tweed coat had partially remained outside, it would seem.

No matter.

After settling back, I just happened to look out to my left as the car moved slowly up the main street to the hotel. I saw three young girls, about eighteen, probably here for the spring skiing. Feeling quite good about things, I leaned gently forward and with a slow, considered backhanded wave, greeted the ladies. Princely style.

They immediately dissolved into gales of laughter.

Maybe it was the coat?

I laughed to myself and sat back. I said to my wife, 'You know, I just cannot believe that those nitwits at the hotel could not get it right!' I reiterated the elements of the situation and became silent.

We rolled up to the front door of the hotel, and the driver turned to me and said, "You should do something about that, sir, you really should!' I said nothing in response but tipped him twice the normal amount. The hotel staff scampered to the taxi to escort us through the main doors to the reception lobby, crammed now with tourists of all shapes, sizes and color from all over the world and beyond. That did not, however, daunt me for NOW! I was 'loaded for bear,' as they say in these parts!

My wife, somehow, evaporated as I shifted up through my gears and stormed through all, to the front of one of the four lines waiting to be received and registered. It was too bad I did not have my kilt on, *that would have helped now*, I thought. I pushed, with appalling manners, two people nosing through the brass bars of the reception desk, to confront a now positively terrified young lady at the other side of the desk. I leaned over about thirty degrees across the brass bars towards her. I said to her, loudly, firmly, but not shouting, 'I want to see the general manager of this establishment; right now, and right here, not in his office.'

The adjacent crowd was shrinking and scattering a bit. The receptionist immediately put her foot on the panic button and a well-dressed young man came out of the paneled wall. There was a ten-second pause. He said, 'I really am sorry, sir, the general manager is golfing at present. I am in charge today.'

Not having cooled off by a long way I said, 'Well, listen lad, this is not your lucky day.'

I explained the problem in thirty seconds. He was shaking a bit by this time, but composed himself fast. He said, 'Follow me, sir.' Grabbing a key from a corner post, he caught his finger in a hinge as he tried to escape to the lobby from behind the reception desk. Suddenly my wife reappeared, aligned at my side, and as we followed the assistant manager to the elevator in haste, she said only, 'Nice clothes in that shop.'

All three of us got into an elevator. We stopped at a floor which I did not know existed. The elevator door opened onto a quaint corridor furnished with some care. Deep rich colors in carpet, drapes and wall hangings, old pieces of furniture easy on the eye, and subdued lighting with a tangerine glow coming from nowhere.

He led the way and stopped soon at an oaken, bronze-bound door, apparently to a tower of some kind. We went up a few spiral steps and stopped at another locked door of similar appearance. He produced the key, old and iron or something, then a modern-looking key, and unlocked the door. A bloody tower, I thought; a damn dungeon in reverse, with a view, perhaps? He opened the door with a cool, dramatic air and said, 'You will both be happy here, sir, it is the honeymoon suite of this hotel.'

Well, now it's two o'clock on an April Saturday afternoon and we have been married for twenty-five years in reasonable harmony and now this proposition? We said nothing while looking around, but he said, with one hand on the door as he was about to leave, 'A bottle of champagne will be sent up to you right away, sir; or perhaps two would be better in the circumstances. Moët, perhaps? We really are very sorry,' he added and left, closing the fairytale door softly.

The room was in a tower with sweeping panoramic views in several directions. It was not a really large room but definitely designed for a specific purpose. There were three main features in the room, compacted comfortably. First, of course, was an enormous bed, a four-poster, draped with beautiful embroidered materials and tasseled all around, with monstrous pillows of silk all over and satin sheets and slips. All this dominated by a white Valentine-like heart in silk as a headboard. At the bottom of the bed and adjacent was a sunken Jacuzzi, about 30 inches deep, six feet in diameter, with racks for, well, towels, drinks and this and that stuff in abundance, but with no rails for easy access. Sit down, slip in routine, *oui*. Across from the arrangement was an elegant oak sideboard, with hammered leather and brass studs. Right couthy, including fruit, chocolates and bottles of wine tastefully placed. Ready for a really nice dinner sent up from the main kitchens of the hotel later.

All very well done, I thought when the champagne arrived, along with our bags and coats from the other, now forgotten, room.

Well, it took the party of the first part and the party of the second part two seconds to decide that we should have a party of the third part. So we opened the champagne and, with tulip glasses in hand, looked the place over. Just magnificent and so intimate, too, no flash, no real excesses, some understandable extravagance, but all good sense. Anybody would be feeling just great in this room for a few hours or a few days. Paradise? Five o'clock now, time of the long shadows, when suddenly the gentle hum of the concealed refrigerator becomes noticeable. A peaceful time of reflection usually. In the distance, on the mountain, cabins now beginning to glow from maple and beech fires and evening skiers now shadowing down trails to the lodge for a mountain evening.

One bottle of champagne was history now; time to order up dinner from the kitchens for seven o'clock. Lest we forget to do so, quite understandably.

We left the second bottle of champagne in the cooler of ice and opened a bottle of sauvignon from California, *c'est bon*, nicely cooled, too, and refreshing with some Melba toast, water biscuits and cheese, gouda and fruit to hold the fort till seven; ah, Saturday spring night approaching, a Canadian sunset by special order coming right up to the first range of the mountains.

'Wonder what we did to deserve all this,' my wife said now, very relaxed, sipping her wine slowly. 'Must have been something I said,' I intoned with limited depth. 'Can't remember what it might have been, either,' I said with equal perception.

I had to bite my tongue when I was about to say, 'I wonder what's on television up here?' I didn't, and opened a bottle of rosé instead, pouring myself a goodly measure.

'Do you remember when we went on our honeymoon to Torquay in England, twenty five-years ago?' she said.

'No, can't say I do.' I replied. 'Much.'

'I liked the Devon cider, though, and their concept of playing cricket.'

Reminiscing about a deckchair in the Channel sun, ham and mustard sandwiches and a good flagon of cooled local cider. She decided not to pursue the subject further, thankfully. There was a knock at the door then, like a furry paw and a very nice, gloved, older man came in with a grin and large pewter tray, to be followed in a few seconds by a second, younger man with a silver tray and a smile. No mountains of food on these servers; individual dishes with local fish and game *mode Français*. Everything exactly right. A one hundred percent recovery performance!

We finished the wine and dinner and opened the other bottle of champagne.

My wife said, 'Oh, to hell with it, let's get in!' pointing to the jacuzzi. She began to fill it with water and pink bath salts of some kind. She said 'Come on,' shedding her skins, all but one and grabbing the champagne bottle. 'Bloody good idea!' said I, somewhat unthinkingly. After about a half an hour and both finishing the champagne, she was beginning to wallow and roll a bit in the heavy seas of the tub, so I said to her, 'My dear, I think we had better get out of this bath and into bed while we both can.'

No reply, I think. She took on a heavy list as I prepared to get out of the bath tub. But certainly helping all that she could. Now the bottom of the bath tub to the top of the adjacent satin sheets was almost six feet and there were no handrails. Just me, status quo. The bed and pillows might just as well be at the top of the Matterhorn as far as she was concerned.

Now, if you think that you have been around the Horn of Life, just you tell me just how do you get a slippery, soapy mermaid-like fifty-year-old, disoriented but delightful, creature into that satin-sheeted bed? Mannerly?

Then I will tell you.

THE NORTHEASTER ISLAND

How can you not go?
If you can.
After you've heard them sing of Cape St. Mary's or Bonavista and Trinity Bays.
How can you not go?
To see the breaking of day over Placentia Bay.
Where the world changed forever.
If you can.
How can you not go?
To stand in the British batteries.
Where history was made many times a thousand feet above St. John's harbor.
Where waves the size of houses crash and break two hundred feet up the cliffs, under a clear blue sky after a storm in the Atlantic.
How can you not go?
If you can.
I found a way, so I could go to Newfoundland.
You should find a way, too, for now; at least a bit of a way.

'It's ten past twelve, sir,' the airport official said cheerfully. 'On a Monday morning or a Sunday night, depending on your point of view.' He added, 'You are the first person to get to St. John's this week on business, so we want to give you a little memento!'

He then gave me a small folding zippered travel bag which I still have.

'Well, that's very nice of you,' I said, accepting the gift and adding, teasingly and knowing the local humor, just a bit, 'Does that mean that you only want me to stay overnight then?'

'No, no, sir,' he quickly replied. 'Now you can take a little something back to Toronto with you in your new bag!'

'I will do that,' I responded sincerely. 'Maybe some of your dark rum, then, that's good for blowing up tree stumps; or maybe some of that special port which you keep in the caves near the harbor just for yourselves!'

'Oi say you've been here before, sur!' he said, lapsing into a seaborne Irish sort of uprooted accent, eroded by time.

'Then welcome back, sur!' he immediately followed, with a certain pride. 'Welcome to St. John's, Newfoundland!' he added.

'Oi'l say you to your taxi, sur,' I said. 'Thank you very much. I see that the warmth of your welcome would still melt the icebergs in St. John's harbor!'

He smiled and closed the door of the car, beaming from ear to ear, knowing that he had caught a live one in his net; five hours before the sun came off the eastern Atlantic horizon.

The only time to catch big fish.

As we passed the road to Portugal Cove in the dark, I thought, *well, you can never really speak the language here unless you are born 'on the rock', but it does help to know the passwords.*

On this visit, I was going to St. Lawrence on the tip of the Burin Peninsula to visit a mine taking fluorspar from under the Atlantic with some difficulty.

I did, and it was no place underground for man, woman or anything else, and they had a cemetery full of people as if to prove it. I thought at the time that it was a strange facet of Newfoundland life, still associated with sea but not in the right way. I was glad to hear that it closed some years later. Good enough for the past maybe, but for future generations better gone, I say.

Since me and mine had been in many such mines, I then felt deeply for the miners and their families having to work such a place, for want of a better choice.

To prevent any melancholy which I might feel, then, with me for the visit, I had Puncher Lambert, who wanted me to see the other side of Newfoundland life, for a day or two.

Puncher was six feet three inches tall, of good nature, and a joy to be with on the return journey by car back up the Burin Peninsula and across to St. John's.

We took the long way home to St. John's and I quickly found out that any way is the long way, if you don't have a good boat and a fair sea. We had only a car. Where the road, twisting along the coast, compels you to watch the scenery and the road ahead, just in case it's not there as planned. Winter is not long over and the new calendars have wafted back onto the walls in some of the draftier places around the bay.

It was a beautiful morning to drive to St. John's on this visit, so we stopped frequently at places of interest and for refreshments. More of the latter as we got closer to home, it would seem, and fitting, too!

On our right hand side was the long bright sparkle of the sun on the waters of Placentia Bay; dazzling across the waves coming from the Avalon peninsula to the east. This must be a far cry from the drab gray and foggy dawn which rose on the British and American battleships, cruisers and escorts, I thought.

So that men of war, searching for peace, could talk safely in Plancentia Bay and change the world forever. Just sixty years ago?

They came.

Now outports, small fishing villages along the bay, their appearance much the same today as then; but futures soon to change with the elusive fish and the ocean open to, well, 'people from away', far away. Now, though, with codfish drying in the spring sun on the dock. Close by, blue and white painted wooden-framed houses with white fences protecting masses of purple lupins, bounding and swaying about in the strong breeze. I turned to Puncher and said, eyeing one of the cottages as the white lace curtains moved, 'I think we are being watched!'

'Oh, yes,' he said, without turning his head, 'they've been watching us since we came over the hill!' And he added with a smile, 'let's have some fun with them, it'll "broiten" up their day and give them a story to tell, sittin' on the dock!' He stopped the car in front of the shipshape and tidy cottage and we got out and he produced a long steel measuring tape from his windbreaker jacket.

'We'll pretend to measure their place up; you take the back of the tape.' With that he scampered off along the white fence, while I put on my surveyor's 'faraway look' and followed.

We more or less ran round the fence and house and we could hear them bumping and knocking over furniture as they tried to traverse round the rooms to get to all the windows in time. Lace curtains waving everywhere just like flag signals at sea; then... by the time we got back to the cottage front door, our sides were sore with laughing!

Puncher said breathlessly, 'I'll go and talk to them now. You stay at the car. Bit of a laugh, eh!' He did do that, and I still do not know what was said to bring forth howls of laughter from the doorway. It was probably about me, and if it was then I'm glad to think so. He got back into the car, said nothing and drove back up over the hill and on up the coast road for about half an hour or maybe more. Then he stopped the car, reached into the back seat and picked up a box with a packet of sandwiches and two bottles of beer. He also reached for a big aluminum pot.

'Let's go up the hill, see the view and pick some partridgeberries,' he said, grabbing for two pairs of boots. We put the boots on and started out across gently sloping moorland to the hill. I stopped quickly after almost bumping into a big steel post with a big red marker, both strangely out of place, I thought.

'Oh, you'll be wondering what that is,' said Puncher. 'You've got your hands on American property there, boy! That there is the buried hotline from America to Russia, used before the satellites!' he announced.

I responded, 'Good God, Puncher, you can't be serious, are you? A Newfoundlander on his way home with a jar of rum inside himself and ten dollars worth of blasting powder could have, well, blown their conversation into Placentia Bay across there!'

'That's true, and they probably tried more than just a few times. Who knows?'

He added, 'Here's the partridgeberries, starting from here up the slope to the top. We'll fill the pot up for my wife. She is going to make a sauce for your dinner with some moose meat that I have. You'll enjoy that, I think!'

'But, Puncher,' I said, 'I'm expected at the hotel for dinner.'

'No you're not,' he said, 'you're coming home with me, we'll have some rum and you can sleep with the dog in the cellar.'

Which I did, all of it.

On the morning after breakfast, Puncher said, 'Tell you what. We'll go out to Cape Spear; the wind there will blow the cobwebs clear from your mind. The northeasters are still blowin' out there, you know. I'll drive you out to the airport later.'

So after thanking his wife for the excellent dinner and hospitality, we drove out to the most exposed and easterly point in North America.

'Europe, eighteen hundred miles that way!' says Puncher, pointing straight out to sea where the waves rolled onto the rocks below the lighthouse. 'Hard to believe that we are also nine hundred miles further east than New York!' he mused.

'During the war, we used to get some German submarines around here. One fired a torpedo through the open defense booms at the entrance to St. John's Harbor.' he said. 'Just to

12

see if we were awake, no doubt! Bloody cheek, eh! They were an audacious lot, you know; our fishermen used to pull them out the water with tickets to the local cinema in their pockets, and that's a fact! Newfoundland, in those days, was a big American communications center for the north Atlantic. People soon forget what happened. Some of us don't,' he rambled on, 'Makes you wonder! Who remembers? What about the young men and women ferrying planes to Europe from here; if they missed a beacon in Scotland to make a right turn, they were gone!'

'We remember all the stories here, lots, you know,' Puncher said, 'We remember,' drifting into a seaward moment's silence. Turning to walk back up the steep path to the car, he just said, simply, 'You also know some of the stories now, maybe some day you'll try to tell them?'

We drove out to the airport just as the plane landed and I had enough time to take my new bag and get some 'small mindings' of Newfoundland, including some lobsters and the special port, thinking again of my welcome to St. John's.

'I'll say goodbye then,' said Puncher Lambert, just a bit sadly, I thought, and he added. 'I meant to get you a small gift, but we're having such a good time it, well, just slipped my mind.'

'Not to worry, Puncher,' I replied. 'Happy memories, like your stories, are by far the best gift.'

I can keep them forever.

THE BEGINNINGS OF A MONEYMAKER

A long time ago I worked for seven years in underground coal mines and it was there that I met Jeem the Miserable.

Jeem looked, acted and thought just like his nickname sounds.

On reflection, we had an interesting group that night thirty-five years ago, who were assembled to carry out an underground survey of the *Lady Veronica* shaft, that curiously formal name for a dingy, damp and dangerous vertical hole in the ground, eighteen hundred cold and dripping feet straight down.

In charge was a capable fellow by the name of Bobby Sharpe. Another grimy face was owned by a young man who later became a prominent politician or something a bit more important, and there was myself and, of course, Jeem the Miserable.

We had just finished a spell underground and we came back up to the surface at dawn to rest a bit and have something to eat prior to returning to the job underground. It had been a very uncomfortable night, cold, wet and generally a bit depressing trying to operate in such cramped and dangerous workings underground. Our cold cheese sandwiches were welcome but not all that inviting, even with the prospect of hot coffee and a seat beside a hot stove.

Bobby, being more affluent at this time than either me or the politician-to-be, decided that he was going to have a hot meat pie, and using the never stated chain of command, ordered Jeem the Miserable to go to the canteen for him.

Jeem was a pathetic soul at the best of times, with a junior Fagin-like appearance. However, a real sight to behold on a bitterly cold dawn. He was iced with dirt and grime from underground and still studiously trying to avoid work as he did all night in that unfortunate place. Bobby gave him a silver coin so he could buy the hot meat pie and, in a moment of weakness, felt sorry for this miserable sight, handing him a second silver coin, to get a hot meat pie for himself, thinking this might cheer up this pathetic soul. (Don't you feel sorry for him!)

Well, Jeem brightened up, or at least as much as he was able, and scampered off to the canteen in the cold wet drizzle.

The politician-to-be and I, who were now chewing gratefully on our dry cheese sandwiches, looked at each other knowingly and without a word, waiting to see how Jeem would handle this situation.

We knew for sure that it would be one for the book.

Well, five minutes later, the door swung open and there was Jeem the Miserable like a drowned rainy rat, and he squeaked 'Bobby, I was running back from the canteen when I slipped on the ice and dropped your meat pie in the mud.'

The politician-to-be choked on his cheddar and I spilled my coffee on my lap. The sometimes priceless Jeem was at it again, we both thought, and it was starting to get real interesting!

Bobby, the ever-patient Bobby, paused, sighed, glanced silently sideways at me and the politician-to-be and said 'Okay, Jeem, it is slippery and the weather is bad this morning and we're all tired,' so he gave Jeem another silver coin and said 'Okay, Jeem, go and get me another meat pie.' Jeem's own pie placed quickly upon entry and now sizzling on the pot bellied stove was never the subject of comment.

Well, Jeem the Miserable took off through the door into the yard to where (we learned later) he dropped the first meat pie. He had picked it up, scraped the icy mud off the greasepaper, pocketed the third silver coin, returned with the ill-fated but passable pie to Bobby and without a blush munched his pie which he had left warming on the black stove.

Jeem the Miserable had his title confirmed!

SCISSORS ARE FOR APRON STRINGS

'I cannot understand it! Why would anyone like you leave all your family, friends and a good job, too?'

'Well, Hammy, there's nae room for us 'a tae picnic at Aberdour. Besides, it's expected of me, and I am ready, well suited and prepared, too! To emigrate that is,' I said to my coal dust friend.

'In my opinion, it's all that simple,' I continued, 'in Scotland.'

'Those that are, should and, those that are not, should not.'

'Besides,' I said, *'you've got to want to go there*, to make different things happen. Anywhere.

'So I'm going there, and I'm going to stay there. It's our choice to make. As a matter of fact, we are both going there, to Canada.

'Bloody exciting, isn't it? We haven't a clue really who we are going to meet, where we are going to stay or even what our family will look like. Bloody exciting, I say!

'Oh look, there's the Denmark Strait down there! Wow! The passage of many good men and great ships! Just a terrible place I've been told.'

God, listen to the wail of that siren in the night snow. Somebody's in trouble out there, I wish I could help.

It's even lonelier than the sound of that train whistle leaving Quebec, I won't forget that! Wonderful people, train men! They seem to understand things.

Now look at that street with light stretching about thirty miles from King Eddie's Tower! To a surveyor's north, I'll bet! Imagine! Swamp, black flies and heat. Good lads!

Well, I've got a job to go to tomorrow, only a mile from here.

That's a good start. *Lucky.*

I wonder if I can design highways? Well. We will soon see. I'll have to start looking for a home for us and a hospital, too, by autumn. Boy or girl, I wonder?

Girl, I think.

I mustn't forget to write back to them and tell them about that now. They will be surprised but pleased.

It's too bad there was just no other way.

I wonder when spring comes here?

We'll need to watch that cold here, though, it's different and dangerous. Must be careful!

Well, Hammy, we're on! Ready or not.

This is our stage!

A STRANGE NOISE AT THE DOOR

One winter evening, with the snow blowing and swirling past our window, Grandma and Grampa were quietly reading in our big comfortable chairs. We were home in our cottage in the country, by the lake and not far from the woods where the wild animals live.

Suddenly, it just seemed, we heard a very unusual sound. A sort of soft but deliberate banging at our side door.

We do have three cats but all were sitting quietly on the floor with their ears up and looking at the door, wondering who this visitor was on such a cold and snowy night.

'Grampa, I think you should find out who is at our door at this time of night,' said Grandma, nodding in her big chair and laying down her book on her table piled with stuff.

I walked quietly across the room, followed by our cautious cats at a distance.

I carefully opened the door and to, my surprise, there was the biggest cat I ever saw, he was standing up on his two hind legs and he held out his great big paw.

'Paws is my name; gentleman GP Paws at your service, sir.'

I was so surprised, I could hardly speak. Finally I said, 'Well, Mr. Paws, that is very interesting and also somewhat puzzling, but what do you want from me on a night like this?'

'Having introduced myself personally, allow me to do so professionally,' said Mr. Paws. 'Sir, I have a license right here in my paw from Leeds county to catch mice and wild things, night and day, and I am trying to find steady work on this bitterly cold night.'

I said, 'Mr. Paws, I do not question your skills and good intentions, but I already have three cats, as you can see, and I don't need any more,'

'Well, yes, that may be true, if I may say so sir, and a well-taken point I might add, but as I understand it from the local cat office, you feed them three meals a day and this renders them ineffective, if not a total washout, at the mouse-catching caper, as we say in the business.' He moved nosily to the top step, sweeping his big yellow eyes through the kitchen behind me, and placed a whopping big paw in the door.

I said, 'Now wait a minute, Mr. Paws, just exactly who are you and what do you want?'

'Genghis Penghis Paws, at your service. President of Catscam Incorporated!' he said, puffing up his white and ginger fur and presenting me with his business card.

I was quite taken aback but said, 'I must admit that you are a most gentlemanly and well-spoken cat, Mr. Paws, but I already told you, I do not need another cat, I do have three very good cats.'

'Well,' said GP Paws, 'That may be true but, respectfully speaking, that is not nearly enough, especially since I am, unlike them, fully qualified to chase away elephants and other things, too.'

'But Mr. Paws,' I said, 'We don't have any elephants in Leeds county, or giraffes either!'

'Well, how about foxes then?' said Mr. Paws, his big round yellow eyes closing to slits.

'Yes,' I said, 'We really do have foxes!'

'Aha!' said Mr. Paws triumphantly. 'Well, sir, how often do you see them there foxes?' Once again he swept his eyes around the kitchen behind me.

I thought for a second or two and replied, 'Oh, about every two or three days I should say, especially in winter.'

He looked at me, rubbing his paw against his whiskers this and that way. 'Every two or three days, sir, very suspicious, as we say in the trade, very, very suspicious! Especially at this time of year', he added thoughtfully. 'May I ask, sir, just how long and tall these foxes are, including that stupid-looking bushy tail? No disrespect to the fox, sir, beautiful animals to have running around wild on your fine property. Bite your grandchildren, they will, though.' He added cautiously.

'How long are they? Oh, some about this long,' I said, stretching my arms out wide.

Paws looked at me and said, 'My goodness, that is big all right, are you sure this was a fox?'

'Yes, I'm sure,' I replied quickly.

'Well, you can't be too careful, sir; back in '86 I skillfully cornered a mangy brush wolf dressed up in a fox suit, ate the fox first, he did. Well, sir, to get back to business, recently, actually quite recently, I should say, I was appointed as Official Fox Relocation Officer for the county of Leeds,' continued Mr. Paws. 'It's more than likely that I can do something for you before he eats your cats.'

'Eats my cats,' I roared. 'Paws, foxes do not eat cats, as you very well know.'

'Well, sir, that used to be the case in the old days, but times have changed, especially in winter,' he said most firmly. 'In fact, there is a fully documented case in Lanark county where such a terrible event took place; fox did not even spit out the fur, I understand from my cousin Dougal Paws Esquire.'

'Really, Mr. Paws, you are going to extremes, are you not?'

'Not at all, sir, not at all,' he said, now gazing through my legs at the goose steaming on the kitchen table. 'Well, sir, let us get back to business, shall we?' He stood up again with just a little impatience, I thought.

'My agent, sorry, my aunt, sir, told me that you have far too many birds around this property in the spring, especially those dirty big crows and turkey vultures,' he stated. 'Maybe I could help in that regard, having run off both species from

Northumberland county back in '89, with the help of a few associates. Got a medal for that, I did,' he added, puffing up his fur.

'Now wait a minute, Mr. Paws, I did not realize cats had associates!' I responded with surprise.

He looked at me carefully and said, 'Well, no disrespect, sir, but there is a lot you do not know about cats, especially one such as I with immaculate qualifications, ready to take on the enemy and perform fearlessly in your back field!' He puffed himself up again. 'Make 'em run up the white flag at the golf course wall is my initial strategy,' he added, looking at me strangely.

I looked this great big cat up and down as he stood high on his back legs and I said, 'Mr. Paws, I do believe you are hiding something from me. Are you not?'

He looked at me with a grin, quite a grin, and said, 'Well, to be totally and completely honest with you, sir, I do have the aforementioned associates on hand,' he glanced at the door to the garden and the deep snow.

'My associates are actually my sisters, sir; my backup boys I calls them, bit more steam to it,' says Paws. 'We are all orphans, so I looks after them, you might say.' Looking me in the eye he said, 'Sir, all we ask is a bed for the night, any corner will do, and perhaps a small snack; leftovers, perhaps? I'm afraid they are quite a sad-looking lot this night, all wet and cold,' he added, glancing at me again. 'Fell in the creek, they did, a terrible affair, first one tripped on my foot, then they all went in like dominoes, sir;' and with that comment and cue in trooped three cats, line astern, all spaced out from the garden and all just half the size of Paws.

'Let me introduce my associates, sir, may I?' he added pointedly. 'This here first cat is called Prize, a bit fat, perhaps pudgy is a rather kinder word, sadly orphaned early and with an all gray fur coat. A touch of class, I would say. C'mon, Prize, move it,' he whispered, facing away from me.

'Sir, Prize's real strength lies in the quaint gray color. You see, when we are sneaking up on these wild beasts on a damp morning, she goes out in front. Perhaps I should point out to you that these are the same wild beasts with the big red eyes that watch you in the night, threatening your household, sir,' he said making his point.

The gray cat then sat down behind Paws.

'Now, sir, I really am particularly proud of the quite subtle skills of this next cat. Charm we calls her, all black, white and ginger, perfect camouflage and social compromise in our game, sorry, our business, sir,' he added. 'She is my persuader, you might say; she tries to talk these wild things into giving up and leaving town before we corners them as a team. A difficult task, sir, a very difficult task, she has!'

And Charm took her place behind Prize, who was now on the second step.

I'm afraid I did not know what to say and Paws did not give me much chance.

'Now, sir, the sort of disoriented, sharp but strange-colored cat coming through your garden door backwards is curiously called Pixie Poo; she is our payload specialist, *and* she always carries a screwdriver, sir, always carries a screwdriver. She goes after the more intellectual type rodents who will chew up the electrical wire and brake cables in your good lady wife's car. They actually enjoys them things, I understand, sir, somehow gets a buzz on, it seems,' he added once again, not letting me get a word in.

'Well, there they are, sir, cute as the buttons on your fine shirt, all licensed operators and performance-oriented.' He pointed to the sorry lot.

'Of course, sir, we only work on one-day contracts and without a pause, if you'll permit me some cat humor on a cold night,' says Paws.

'We are ready to start now, sir, or soon, and no wages or benefits, how can you get a better deal than that in today's world?' Paws stood fully upon his back paws peering almost across my shoulder into the warm kitchen and sniffing from side to side.

'Well, Mr. Paws', I said. 'You do present your case quite well, perhaps you and your associates had better come in from the cold night air.'

Paws beamed from ear to ear, dusting his whiskers from side to side with his big paw.

'We are most honored by you consideration, kindness and hospitality, sir. I hope you will not think it forward or presumptuous of me if I politely enquire what are the arrangements for supper today? Not too much gravy on the goose, sir, must leave room for the wild things.'

Just at that point a cold strange shiver ran through me like the draft from a closing door.

'What was the noise at the side door?' said Grandma, pulling her warm wooly winter shawl around her.

'It was just the north wind, Grandma; just the north wind,' I said, slowly rising from my big chair, smiling.

'Smiling just a bit?'

SEEING IS BELIEVING – BUT NOT ALWAYS

Although this is the sixth story in this collection of short stories, this is the last story written out of the thirty voyages into the past and the world of imagination constructed to varying degrees around a framework of truth. I have been involved, personally, one way or the other in all the experiences recounted. I do have a big cat called Genghis Paws. Only the fourteenth story and the twenty-ninth story are purely imaginative, at least I think they are. Who am I to say? The reason why this short story has taken so long to crystallize is that the idea for the basic story, well, I kept forgetting. When I finally remembered I made some notes, then I lost my notes twice, and my impatience then made me lose my interest, three times or more. I always seem to be losing something.

'Missing…' 'Not there?' Just disappearing.

'Disappearing' is a useful and better word. Candle-like, as a will-o'-the-wisp, off and on in the marshland dark. We know it has one atom of carbon and four atoms of hydrogen and mystery, too. A blue–yellow flicker of light. It's my there again, *gone again mist*, as mentioned in another story.

Gone again mist is a product of observation, age and experience and is to some degree a sweeping magician's cloak given to almost everybody eventually, in some form.

We remember what we want to remember, or not, and we see what we want to see, or not!

I remember this story well, too well, because it's true! I HAVE TRIED TO FORGET IT, BUT I CAN'T!

In Ontario we have a marvelous catchall phrase for all sorts of mists, fogs and inadequacies.

It's called 'the lake effect'.

It was conjured up by weather forecasters to explain unexplainable aberrations in weather conditions along the shores of Lake Ontario. More snow, less snow, more sun, less sun, more rain, less rain.

Gone again mist is not unique to Lake Ontario, oh, no! My goodness no. Other varieties exist in Bermuda, Lake Okanagan in British Columbia, Lake Memphromagog in Quebec and, of course, Loch Ness in Scotland and all over the latter in general. What was Brigadoon after all, besides charming?

The last three, of course, are more specialized mists and relate to people and water horses or something.

The lake effect in Ontario is quite a different mist, being a function and spin of a force so great that it makes all kinds of things just disappear, just whisked away like the magician's silk in a swoop!

I tell you – people and things just vanish!

I didn't know about the lake effect when I arrived in Canada forty years ago, but I definitely knew there was something very strange going on. At that time, and volumes have been written about the mystery, Canadians were chopping up, literally, an entire potential squadron of beautiful batwing fighter aircraft with the highest performance figures in the world.

Yes, really. Someone told someone to do so for some reason.

Well, right away I knew there was much more to it all than that. It seemed to me so bizarre and beyond all ken that it had to be the effect of *gone again mist* on people and things.

After all, I had seen the stuff before at Urquhart Castle on the north shore of Loch Ness but the mist on the north shore of Lake Ontario was of a technological nature, sort of.

Down falls the colorful silk, under a gray screen, and something disappears right before your eyes! PRESTO!

When the airplanes disappeared we did have a bluff prime minister who looked alarmingly like everyone's idea of an impresario, especially in a cape. *Gone again mist* eventually got to his entire party much later. It had happened before, too! But not in Canada.

Even more strange and curious to me at the time, this trick was widely used by another prime minister, who well understood the magic effect of properly salted *gone again mist* on both people and things; a force way beyond the triviality of mere spin. He scared the hell out of his own people and Americans, too, by appropriating and wearing cloaked silk and a wide brimmed hat; plus beautiful assistants, too, here and there. Always a dead giveaway.

However, practising *gone again misters* eventually can't resist dressing up and disappearing themselves, sometimes to reappear on the tennis court at the Southampton Princess Hotel in Bermuda, or some such place. Needless to say, in their real get up, applying topspin to a helpless wee ball.

It was November and the city of Toronto was blanketed by a fog which had rolled in from Lake Ontario. I thought that it was just the foggy, foggy dew from America, but maybe it wasn't.

Once again I was sitting in my Toronto office.

The phone rang and I said to myself, 'God, not another story I'm going to have to try to remember?'

It was.

Gone again mist had found out that I was in town and a likely candidate for a mystery. I was in the steel business at that time, helping the Italians to build today's Toronto, which was a pleasurable task from start to finish.

Alexander Charles Ruffus Puffin was, without a doubt, an engineer's engineer, as they say. Red hair to match his name and temperament! He disappeared along with several associates overnight. One day he was there and the next day he was not there. He was an electromechanical engineer – a very, very good one too! He was on the other end of the phone that day. Alex said, 'I hear that you know something about spirally welded steel tubes?'

'A bit,' I said. 'We use them for piled building foundations and special water transmission lines.'

'I have something quite different in mind. Could you come down so that we can talk about it?' he asked. I said that I would be pleased to do so and I would come down in the afternoon. He described an area downtown close to the new developments, near the railway tracks and in an area of old warehouse buildings. Many were empty at that time.

I drove down in the early afternoon. The fog had lifted and been replaced by sleet and early snow. A dirty November day, like those of northern Europe. Not inspiring weather at all!

I had a feeling that the visit would prove interesting. I don't know why, but I just felt that way.

When I got there and parked my car, the downtown high-rise buildings were almost hidden by the snow and sleet driving off the lake by an easterly wind carried one thousand miles from the Atlantic. I parked the car and got my briefcase from the backseat, put my collar up and leaned into the driving snow. The address was a five-story redbrick building and it looked empty, except for the top floor where all the windows glowed with yellow light. It looked as if the entire top floor was open space, which it was, about six thousand square feet of it.

I went through the glass doors into a very shabby lobby with worn linoleum. One couch by the elevator and one low table, both as shabby as the lobby itself.

I went to the elevator and noticed the indicator was showing five and on the panel buttons, one light glowed next to a new stainless brushed aluminum sign; it said simply, 'Nexus Systems'.

I went into the elevator and up to the fifth floor; it was open, entirely as I had thought, since all the windows were lit up. There was no doubt in my mind what this was. It was an engineering laboratory; a dozen benches with half a dozen engineers or scientists in buff-colored laboratory coats. Alex and his red hair stood out. He was the boss man. He strode across to the elevator, stretched out his hand as if he had been waiting for me and in a Buchan coast accent said, 'Have I got something to show you!'

As we walked to one of the benches he just said, 'We are all problem solvers here and we are all British; that's why we phoned you!'

I said to Alex, 'What sort of problems do you solve?'

'Oh,' he said, 'All sorts of things. Even some weapons technology, torpedoes, guidance systems. Anything interesting, really; a problem not yet solved is our business, nothing else. Despite these surroundings, we get very well paid.' He whispered, 'Mostly in US dollars too!'

I said to him that my field was really mining and civil engineering as it relates to applications for Canadian steel.

'Then you're the very man we need!' he said.

He asked me first about short concentric steel tubes. He wanted to know about the manufacturing method and strength of the automatically welded joints. His emphasis was on high-temperature exposure of the steel and the effect of vibration. I told him what I knew and phoned a design engineer at a factory north of Toronto to verify specific properties of the basic steel coil prior to fabrication into a spirally welded tube.

Alex was satisfied with the information, then he got up from his chair, got everyone's attention and just said, 'Open all the windows, gentlemen, please!'

His associates leapfrogged around the entire floor opening the windows.

The cold gale from the Lake scattered papers and made me turn up my collar again. The six or seven men put on winter parkas and returned to their respective benches. Alex ushered me to a bench about ten feet long and five feet wide. The bench was of heavy wood. Upon it was a device which looked like a solenoid, a steel tube wrapped with electrical wire. On looking closer it was actually three or four concentric steel tubes; one inside the other. At one end of the device was a transformer for changing voltage and perhaps varying resistance to electric current; it was a dual purpose electrical control system of sorts. Somewhat crude.

At the other end was a makeshift control panel with a few dials and switches, also a large and prominent temperature gauge measuring room temperature but also measuring various spot temperatures by electrodes tack welded to various parts of all of the pipes and then to a dozen or so small temperature gauges. He waited for about fifteen minutes and then shouted, 'Close the windows, please!' His associates scattered and closed all the windows. Then he said, 'Shut off all the steam radiators, please,' and half a dozen pairs of hands turned the radiators to the off position. Then he turned to me and said, 'What's the room temperature now?'

I looked at the mercury on the gauge and I said, 'Alex, the temperature in the center of this room is forty two degrees Fahrenheit.'

'Correct,' he said. 'Now watch.'

He threw a circuit breaker switch and said, 'Let's take a walk around the room for a bit.'

I said, 'Okay, I give up, what is the device?'

He said, 'It's a cheap, efficient electric furnace for domestic or industrial heating. That's the prototype. The oil companies will be as mad as hell when they find out about it!'

'Hell, Alex,' I said, 'the biggest electricity authority in the bloody world, pretty well, is just up the road; you can't lose.'

'Maybe, maybe not,' he said. After fifteen minutes we went back to his bench and he said, 'What's the temperature now then?'

I looked at the gauge and it said 64°F.

I said, 'Alex, this is impossible, these tubes would be red hot by now to radiate the entire room temperature by 22° in fifteen minutes!'

He just said, in his Scottish burr, 'Well they're not, are they?'

'Good God, Alex,' I said, 'Do you realize what you have? A bloody tiger by the tail!'

'Nice analogy,' he said, 'and it's true, We have built something which has never been done before, anywhere!'

All the time, while in his presence, I felt, and strangely, that I was there not to give advice and technical guidance on steel tube design. He seemed to know all that much better than I did; I felt I was invited to see this device to bear witness to its operation for some reason. This was thirty years ago and I have never changed my mind. I saw something very special built by very special people, and I still wonder why.

Two weeks later I phoned him to see if we could do anything further.

The phone was dead.

I got into my car and drove the few miles to the laboratory and went up in the elevator.

The room, or floor rather, was completely empty. It was absolutely eerie as I walked around.

There were no benches, no equipment, no wires or cables. Not a solitary item on the entire floor. Not even a wastebasket. Absolutely nothing! Everything gone!

I knelt down and drew my finger across the floor, and also on the window sill. There was no dust at all. The place had been totally cleared and vacuumed throughout! Not a landlord tidying up, a professional exit job! No traces!

I went down to my car, drove onto the street and switched my headlights on and drove off into the densest fog I had seen for years in Toronto.

'This is ridiculous!' I said to myself, peering into the gray mist.

'Mist.' 'Fog.' 'Just like a cloak!'

'Even feels mysterious!'
'Can't see a thing.'
'Didn't even say goodbye.'
'MUST BE.'
'Same again.'
'Gone again!'

'Well, I told him.'
'Marcus Flavius,' I said, 'If you go with the Ninth Legion into that awful fog, in that terrible country, that will be the end of it for you.'
'Mark my words. Gone again!'
'Always the same.'
'Nobody listens to me. No empathy. No recall.'
'Think I'm making it up, do you?'
'Should have stayed in Spain, Marcus,' I said.
'Nice there.'
'Even Africa was better!'
'No, I can't get you a transfer,' I told him. 'What do you think I am, Marcus? A magician or something?' I asked.

LETTERS TO SASKATCHEWAN

Two headstones from the shield and a lifetime away, friends
now to the west wind. Stones of black, blossom-dusted in the
spring breeze; polished for survival.

Two stones, together, backs to the rim.

My God! A house fortressed by a high hedge against the
wind!

'Excuse me, is your name Hamilton?'

'It is,' said the lad most sparingly.

Nothing has changed in us, I see.

'Then I know who you must be.'

'Hullo,' the woman said with a rustle, as if she'd been
expecting me, brushing the wisps of gray, ready to speak again.

'I've come a long way to see you and it's taken a very long
time.'

She didn't invite me in. I think I know why.

'I'm from near the other Tantallon.'

'You're Scottish, then?'

'Yes, I am.'

'I have the letters in a box and have kept them now for over
fifty years,' she soon said, pausing. 'No one really knew her
first name here, she was called Grannie Sutherland.'

Unsmiling, she was; perhaps well aware that the black stone
was for no others' name.

'*Strange thing* that you should come now,' she said, slowly sweeping the yard with sea-blue eyes which I had watched before, in another time in another person.

'I was going to take down the old house last summer, but I didn't, I don't know why;' her eyes fastened on an old cabin, long surrendered to the wind and now resting peacefully in the raspberries as if its job, too, was done.

So this is Tantallon.

Man, the letters stopped here; letters that as a boy, I saw leave there; a long time ago. Irreplaceable letters, whispers of home, treasured by the stove, passed around at hard-won Christmas tables or perched against brown tea spouts, before the sunblaze came up again. Letters of faith and encouragement, perhaps? Only one person knows, now; not ever me.

Another Grannie, another time, these first dancing blue eyes in a different dress.

Nearby, the old Tantallon was a different place. Stones, too, soft mossy green to a slate sea, where the wind-blast dismantled the masons' craft. Castle stones, this time; foolishly defiant to the troubled east wind.

'Why are you writing these letters?'
'Because I always do.'
'But why?'
'Because I always do.'
'Well, where are they going then?'
'To Tantallon.'
'But there is Tantallon.'
'It's another one.'
'I see.'
'Sometimes, I'll see, Grannie.'
'Stop the car; I want to speak to that old woman in the field.'

'Oh, yes, I know who you mean; they live on top of the valley rim. They came a long time ago, I think they are mostly gone somewhere now.'

Again?

'You'll be wondering what happened to them?' she said, needlessly buttressing the swaying hedge.

'Well, they are across there, behind the lilacs.'

'I still keep all the letters in a drawer you know; you're welcome to see them!'

'No, these letters were never meant for my eyes, but I'm glad to see they got here.'

Oh, how she would have smiled and been pleased to know that.

THE FIRST HOSPITAL CAPER

A few years ago a friend of mine said to me, 'You know some people go through life and nothing interesting ever happens to them.' He was of course placing himself in this category and me in the other.

I have always thought that it was a real shame to take the safe and comfortable course in life since this usually leads to the circumstances he so aptly described. However, it has been my observation that frequently the same experience, so to speak, can happen to each type of person with a totally different interpretation or reflection of what actually took place.

A visit I made to the hospital not so long ago is not a bad example. I'm sure someone like my friend would have seen little of interest and less of the humorous aspect of such an experience. Perhaps it helped to be one of the fortunate people who had managed to keep reasonably clear of hospital after making my original debut some time ago.

Well now, I was going to see what goes on first hand, in a hospital, you might say, since the doctor had suggested I go and have surgery performed on a slight swelling on the wrist known as a ganglion. Well, this seemed to me to be quite a lot of fuss to be made about a wee bump on the wrist, since my Scottish grandmother used to give them a good belt with the dictionary or, more likely, the Bible, to cause them to disappear forthwith. Still, modern medical science might know something that Granny Miller didn't, so I went into the hospital, just as my doctor suggested.

Well, I eventually got registered at the reception and was soon ushered into a small anteroom by a nurse and asked to leave my clothes in a locker and put on a cute green smock and get up on one of those trolleys; which I dutifully did, I must confess, with more curiosity than trepidation. Hell, so far, this was fun!

I thought to myself, it looks like they're going to go through with the whole bit, when one of the nurses swiftly injected a sedative into my arm. This encouraging twist relaxed me quite nicely and was, after ten minutes, a little like the effects of a good Scotch.

I was beginning to think this ain't half bad, and I found myself smiling at the almost friendly-looking ceiling.

Soon an orderly wheeled the trolley along the corridors and I figured that to keep this thing rolling, I might just as well enjoy the experience and see what goes on here. I'll have to admit that the sedative helped and kept me feeling pretty good about most things on that day.

I was then wheeled into a large elevator and up to the third floor and left on the trolley, feeling like a discarded hotel room service order, outside the operating theatre. 'Must be a big day here, lining me up and all that,' said I to myself. Anyway, there I was lying on my back in pretty good shape, but dozing slightly, when I heard some scuffling behind my head and two small boys, probably escaped from some nearby waiting room, walked by, whispering to each other. One said to the other, 'I think he's dead.'

I opened one eye and they took off like to beat hell!

Now the operating theatre was something else again. I could not believe that this performance was for my bump and my benefit; three crispy clean white and striped nurses bustling about, a suspiciously sulky anesthetist, possibly sulky because he had sniffed his own stuff and, of course, the surgeon, wheeling around like a ship in full sail, and the whole place full of whistles, shiny bells and blazing light.

Being more or less the thinking sort, I was cruising through my mind the possibilities of a error here, to my disadvantage, since the stage really did seem to be set for a major performance as I lay strapped helpless to the table, arms spread-eagled to the side supports and not in any real position to ask questions. The sedative and me were well and truly traveling by this time but I was still clinging to the thought about something more serious being removed without my consent.

By this time, the now leering anesthetist was sliding a needle into my right arm and my countdown had started. At a count of ninety-five, the very last thing I saw that sunny spring morning was a curiously smiling nurse, masked revenge in her blue eyes, with soap and a shiny open razor!

'Sheila,' I gasped.

THE EGGBEATER'S FRIEND

Being a bit unusual myself, I tend to be interested in unusual people and especially unusual people in unusual places, doing unusual things.

There is really nothing unusual about this at all.

I don't go looking for unusual people, unusual places, or even unusual events; they just seem to somehow find me and that is usual, usually.

Some time ago, a very unusual friend of mine invited me to lunch. He telephoned to say that perhaps about twelve o'clock, at his place, next Saturday morning, might be a good idea. I said that was just fine and that I would be there. This was quite a usual method of him extending an invitation. The day came and I walked across to his place in a relaxed manner. He was an interesting person and talked about interesting things and he had a priceless sense of humor and what I liked about him was that he was always laughing at himself and also getting into unusual circumstances easily.

When push came to shove he always seemed to be able to trot out some story from his background or experience or even isolate some simple reality somewhat unnoticed before by most.

His wife answered the door! Somewhat cool!

I walked into his place and looked around. Normally he would be right there with two tall glasses of lager to move things right along. At first his wife did not say anything; this was not unusual for her, so I looked around a bit, then she said with total neutrality, 'He is in his bathroom; he is expecting you and lunch is already set up in there.' She picked up a glass with ice-borne Scotch in it, handed it to me and said, shaking her head, 'Up the stairs, second on the left and you better take this bottle of wine with you, too. Just in case,' she added.

I said, 'All right, my dear. What's for lunch?'

'Black forest ham and scalloped potatoes; his favorite,' she said, 'in his bathtub!'

'Oh,' I responded, 'my favorite bathroom lunch, too.'

Maybe if I told you that I was a Scotsman and he was an Englishman, it will visually help a lot here, although we were both Canadians by then. Albeit unusual ones. Perhaps.

I went up the richly carpeted stair, second on the left she said. All doors looked the same, I thought, also that everything was quiet; rather unusual at a luncheon. No matter. Knock knock.

'Enter!' boomed the voice; so I opened the door, turning the brass knob till the door was about a foot open. I stuck my head round the door.

Well I'll be damned; there he was, sitting in his bloody bathtub with an officer's field table next to the bath, upon which was a big brass tray with two bottles of London gin, a bucket of ice and a bottle of Vermouth, also flared martini glasses and some olives, too!

'What's new and exciting?' he said, rubbing his shoulders with a loofah, speaking casually as if he was sitting at the bar of the Chateau Laurier, where he recently fell off a bar stool and broke his arm.

'Not a helluva lot, Roger; what's new with you?' I said, now sitting down on the toilet with nonchalance, and putting my Scotch on the bidet; for which I suddenly grasped the real purpose of the designers! How bloody sensible of them, I thought!

'Hey! What's with the heated toilet seat, Roger?' I said, noting the glow from below.

'Just got fed up looking at a heated towel rail with a cold bottom, old chap!' he said.

I really shouldn't have asked and I sure as hell wasn't going to ask about all the boats floating around in the foam of his bath. He was a delightful fellow, really, but he easily took offense; unusually touchy upon occasion.

'Bit early for Scotch, isn't it?' he said, searching for the soap. 'Sun's in the sky,' he added, nodding at the window.

I said, 'Yes, but not in Scotland,' taking a good charge up to see me through the lunch start-up games. By this time I had noticed a bamboo trolley, a warming tray and some covered stoneware. Lunch?

I thought I would try to spark him up a little by lifting the lid of the bidet and putting the wine bottle in there. He sipped his Martini and said, after a while, 'Interesting comment on my cellar; I thought you would notice.'

'By the way,' I said, 'Roger, what are you doing in your bathtub?'

'Well, I'm having a bath,' he said, 'and thinking.'

'Not about England and St. George and all that, surely?'

'Well,' he said, 'not eggsactly,' he added, somewhat slurring the 'x' for good reason. 'I was thinking about the time they sent me out to see Maude up in Yorkshire. Bit of bother there.'

'Oh, that Maude,' I said, sipping the Scotch and acting as the continuity person.

'Yes, her, the Bloody Eggbeater. Very unusual, she was. Only woman that I ever met who would give you the straight goods with no nonsense.'

'Well, Roger,' I said, 'Yorkshire women are a bit like that, you know; Scarborough especially.' I was teasing him a bit, because I knew that he used to work for a famous British food products company years ago and I think he had said before that they had factories both in the north east of Scotland and also in the north east of England. At that time, as a young man, he had been involved in productivity studies to improve competitiveness in some of their factories.

He had told me a story before, about a food inspector they had for twenty years, who had been in charge of a factory in Aberdeen for smoking herrings and he had stained his skin so dark and so much that he got thrown out of a crusty Edinburgh hotel for telling them he had been a sergeant in the Black Watch in Baluchistan. Roger said he wasn't asked to leave the hotel because of the color of his skin, but because of behavior and the fact that he had admitted to being in the Black Watch while in Edinburgh!

So I knew that Maude, of Yorkshire, must be among his corporate kitchen acquaintances from way back. Somehow!

'Bit violent she was,' he resumed. 'All I asked her was would you please crack those eggs at about half your normal speed, so that we can photograph the sequential process properly. You see, old chap, Maude spent all her morning cracking eggs and separating the yolk from the white. Then she spent all afternoon beating up the whites of the eggs, rather enthusiastically, I thought, too! We used to separate the yolk and egg white for quite different food products.'

I said, 'Very interesting, Roger,' flushing the toilet, 'but why would she be violent, apart from the fact that you were about to make her redundant?'

'Well, it still didn't give her a good reason to bloody well fill my bowler hat halfway full with yolks,' he said.

'Perhaps, Roger,' I said, 'that was all she could think of at the time, with the available weaponry; fight with what's near and handy, name of the game sometimes, don't have time for sophistication, you know! Think of it, Roger, she wasn't angry at you, personally; after all; the violent beating of the egg whites in the afternoon signaled problems at home, perhaps; who really knows? Mustn't judge anybody!'

'Never thought of it that way, old boy,' he said. 'Most inconsiderate of me, really.'

'I say, Roger. You didn't actually put your hat on, did you?'

'No, good heavens, no. I didn't do that! I saw the eggs in the bowler hat, so I picked it up, inverted, of course, in a dignified manner, made a smart about-turn and marched out of the room like the Household Cavalry lookin' for their 'orses!'

'Sort of declared the whole episode a draw! Really, Roger!' I said. 'I don't suppose that this is your way of telling me that you only have eggs now for lunch?'

'Good heavens, no, man, that was my breakfast ham and things! Be a good chap and hand me that bathrobe, will you? We'll be late for lunch! Car coming for us at one o'clock! Take two gins with us. Be at the Chateau at half past one! Get back up on me barstool, old boy! We'll go to Desjardins later. Smoked whitefish all right with you?'

'Just wouldn't have lunch any other way, Roger, old chap!'

'See you downstairs, then! Don't forget the wine!'

THE BLACK TIME BUBBLE

You are going to visit a time bubble and you are not going to
like it very much.

You will be safe, however, since you will be with me.

To go there you cannot be what you are now so you will be
my reflection for a while. We will go to a place where you have
never been before and I will be your guide. You will be in a
time bubble for only thirty seconds. You will be in mortal
danger but possess zero fear, for you have no good reason to be
afraid, have you? And you are with me from now on down.

We now live in the darkness, deep underground, only ten
minutes from a time bubble; we are not afraid because we have
no choices left. Your emotions are now on idle and your
imagination is in gear now. You will gladly exchange the
surreal drift for the very real now if you wish to go further, but
we are not alone now, since there are now six of us and you.
No one is afraid. We are all good at what we do and what we
have to deal with now, for now we are going to deal with and
face up to the worst of all fears, for many. Death by drowning
in a deep, dark and wet underground coal mine. Trapped!

If you are my reflection, you are twenty-two years old, you
are a Scot, and you are a mining surveyor of the deep coal. A
navigator of the dark places. All our companions are the best at
what they do, so you are in safe hands for now and all other
choices are gone. A problem has to be solved. Imagine, we

have two underground coal mines close together; one is new, the other is old. The old abandoned one is full of water, eight hundred feet deep, the other is eight hundred feet plus deep also, and not full of water, as yet. One mine is one hundred years old, the other is ten years old. The reality is that we have a flooded underground city hazarding the lives of three hundred men in a new town. We are going to do something about that right now, and you are coming with me. The way has been prepared for today for three years by tunneling to where we all are now, bent over. You are crowded down in a dark space four feet high and twelve feet wide, cramped, the only light is from headlamps now. The water is up over your ankles and sloshing; it's hot because of poor ventilation air. It is, in effect, raining heavily from the proximity of vast amounts of water and seepage. You are very close to the torrents of water to come; only some coal stands firm now between you and the water and death. The noise is so loud that when you speak you have to shout. So you don't speak much. The noise comes from high speed electric drills in a fan-like pattern around you, probing for the water body. The ventilation fans also, pumping air through flapping canvas tubes, and centrifugal water pumps, holding the black water level at your ankles, are noisy, too.

Behind you are two miles of tunnels out to the surface and daylight; no escape for you now if things went wrong. You are out of choices again. Now you have been asked by the mining engineer, the mechanical engineer and the electrical engineer, 'Where do you think the water is now?' Well, no time for hesitation or lack of confidence for us. You reply that as far as you know, it is within fifty feet and probably on our right hand side somewhere. That what you reply, that's what you say, that's what you have to say, but that is not what you feel or think now, because you know too much, too young. The five others do not, thankfully. You know that a score of collective small errors over a hundred years by maybe dozens of men toying with flimsy trigonometrical probabilities has now come home to roost and a time bubble is forming around you and you can do nothing whatsoever about it now. Since you are there with me, can you hear the deafening noise of the machinery in the confined space and feel the water splashing up all around us? It's very cold if you are there; you can hear the mining engineer say to the soaked mining crew, 'Stop the drilling, shut off the generators, shut down the pumps and slow down the fans – quick as you can.'

So now you hear the noise tangle disappearing until only the water slap-splashing and dripping can be heard. Everyone is silent, only the breathing now. Silence, listening, silence now, listening, silence again, holding silence.

He says now, quite quietly, in the splashing, 'Miners and surveyor to remain, all others must leave the place now.'

So you are staying with me, since, finally, the bubble has now been formed all around us, the last choice has gone, the last door is closed, confluence is now in place, one hundred years in the making.

The engineer continues. 'I want a sixteen foot drill probe at forty-five degrees or so to our right, quickly!'

The black bubble will be burst soon by eight hundred feet, above us, deep water; one way or the other now. It will come under reasonable hole control at extremely high pressure; or that same pressure will break the coal and explode the water into our place and we will be killed by impact soon. At twelve feet, the two miners, suddenly, are blown back by their machines and the force of the water shooting from the hole like a liquid lance, solid, full of stone and dust particles: razors! The lance is forty feet long and soon three inches in diameter and forced between you, me and the engineer.

'Bearing on the water, please!' he shouts. 'Quickly,' he adds.

We move to within twelve inches of the jet, align the crosshair sights of a compass along the jet lance, no thoughts, no fear, just do the job. Three seconds to make the fix and quickly memorize the bearing for records.

'All set, Jimmie,' we say and move aside, but still five feet from the water.

'Plug and secure the place!' he roars.

The two miners, the bravest of the brave, now fight their way to the source of the lance water; no breakage of adjacent coal? Yet! All over soon. God the water up to our knees now. The bubble holds! The plugs hold! The plugs hold! The plugs hold! We all hold! We all hold! *God these people were right, it's impossible, but all these damn people were right,* I said to myself, *how could that be?*

The engineer looks at me and says, 'looks as if we were about right, lad! Let's get out of here and back to the surface,' he adds.

An hour later, we got back to the sun and the surface and as we did so, the manager and engineer turned and said to me, 'You know on that last bit, I felt that there was someone else there, too, besides the four of us.'

I said, 'There was indeed, Jimmie.'

SUMMERDUST

I had always felt that some of the significant differences between English and Scottish law were important, and it says something for those people who ensured that there was indeed a significant difference between the framing processes.

'Not proven,' the verdict, that is, does stick out as a difference north of the Tweed and it was one that seemed to drift through my mind for some reason. I'm really not sure why. I hadn't done anything but it didn't look too good at the time with me and the London bobby.

It is unfortunate that some people like me are absolutely born with a 'latent look' on their faces and are plagued with this problem throughout life. Nobody believes us, right, wrong or anything in between, except at Halloween, perhaps.

I can remember, even as a boy, how a neighbor of ours, an inspector in the local constabulary, always looked at me with some suspicion that more or less said 'guilty before charged,' and then his look transitioned a bit. He was, in fact, a prince of a policeman and if I told you his name, you would never believe it, either. It was Hector Law. Go on, check, I dare you! Ask Harris? Anyway often he perused my person, as above, he then always dissolved into a broad smile as if to say in the Scottish idiom, 'Mind what you are doing!'

However, that is not what was on my mind as I gazed through the cabin window trying to penetrate the 'there-again-gone-again mist' drifting between me and the famous ship. I could even see her guns! I had fallen asleep, and startled by a cabin noise, I had wakened.

It was a beautiful Monday morning and we were cruising up the English Channel with the spring sun just rising like a Dutch cheese popping up from the Netherlands. We flew over Nelson's *Victory* in Portsmouth harbor, courtesy of British Airways. How nice, I thought, and what a grand welcome to England again.

I hadn't had time to put on my 'latent look' yet, so the delightful flight attendant suggested that a cup of tea might help me do that before we got to Heathrow. How very nice again!

I had been in my Toronto office on Friday when the phone rang.

'I hear,' said a polished voice, 'that you know how to build aircraft hangars' (not introducing himself) 'for Boeing 747s.'

I said, 'Yes, that's quite true,' screening my accent a bit.

'I also hear,' he continued, 'that you can build them for a million pounds less and in half the time, according to the videotape I saw. Is that true?'

I replied, 'Yes, that's true, that is quite true. But our aircraft hangars are very ugly.' I added.

'Oh,' said the voice, 'Now why would that be?'

I said, 'Well, as we see it here in Canada, all aircraft hangars are ugly, absolutely all of them. Some ugly hangars have lots of steel sticking out everywhere. Our ugly aircraft hangars don't have any steel sticking out anywhere, so they cost a million pounds less. As a matter of fact we have two ugly hangars at Toronto International Airport and a really ugly hangar at Columbo Airport in Sri Lanka, all built in six months. One was a world record. Satisfied clients, too.'

'Oh, really?' said the managing director from London. 'Well, look here!' he said. 'Come to think of it, we have a really ugly hangar here ourselves in London and it does have lots of steel sticking out of it! And it cost a bloody fortune to put up!' he added, now joining in the advanced technical conversation,

'Do you think that you could come to England right away, Monday, I mean, to a meeting?'

'Why the urgency?' I asked. 'It usually takes some time to plan a hangar layout.' I said, probing for intent and substance.

'Well, it seems it may be too late; but I fear we are about to put up another ugly hangar in the north of England.'

I said, 'This is serious! Like creeping fescue. Well, I can't have these ugly hangars with the steel sticking out spreading into Scotland. Never do! They all know up there that I'm in the ugly hangar business and that's bad enough.'

'Good show,' he said, 'See you Monday morning, then.'

It was extremely hot and humid when I left Toronto and it was almost as hot and humid when I got to London. It was sticky and uncomfortable.

Not to worry.

I knew that I would be all right the second I saw the very nice country hotel as the taxi drew into the courtyard. There was an immaculate English spring garden surrounding the small hotel.

'You must be worn out,' said the host. 'Lunch has been finished. The dining room's empty, sir. I'll set a table by the window for you.'

'Something light to eat, to hold you till later, sir? Gammon sandwich sound good? Hot mustard and pickled onions be all right? Recommend the bitter, sir, two pints and you'll be as right as rain. How's the weather in Canada?'

I couldn't possibly have had a better reception or nicer room than that I had that day. I also saw quickly that the room overlooking the garden was one where the walls had heard many whispers and many accents just not so long ago. Bishop's Stortford was near Stanstead, the old US fortress base northeast of London.

I soon forgot about aircraft hangars and drifted off to sleep in the late afternoon with the window open. I could almost hear the waves of aircraft taking off, in my reverie. Daylight bombing...

The next forty-eight hours were quite hectic before I returned to London and my encounter with the bobby.

I met the managing director, a very nice man and talked to his people about ugly aircraft hangars and he suggested that I go to Leeds to talk to some consultants who didn't think aircraft hangars were ugly; especially theirs. I took the train to Leeds on the Tuesday and arrived at their office, brushing aside the cobwebs with my umbrella and told them what I knew about ugly aircraft hangars.

They thought I had a very interesting, refreshing point of view for a Canadian with a Scottish accent. So there!

They asked me if their client *forced* them to build an ugly cheap hangar rather than an ugly expensive hangar, with a reduced fee, could I, in fact, do so?

I said, 'Yes, I could do this, but I would have to go to a factory in Scotland to be able to give them an accurate cost.' I also said, 'The Scots are quite interested in building ugly aircraft hangars with lots of expensive steel hanging out, but I think that I could persuade them to look at the simple Canadian concept, if need be? It won't be easy,' I added.

I actually did then fly to Edinburgh, where the factory manager picked me up at the airport with his Mercedes.

I told him the whole story and it was not long before we sensibly adjourned to the nearest pub, both knowing that there was no way an ugly hangar was going to enter Scotland.

After a while, looking over the Firth of Forth at South Queensferry, we decided to put together a cost estimate of the aircraft hangar with a definite strategy that perhaps if we allowed one more expensive ugly hangar to be built in Manchester then we could prevent the spread to Scotland.

It was built, it is there and it is definitely ugly, and expensive.

As we were capsulizing our strategy and looking across at the Forth bridge, I said, 'Alex, when I got to Heathrow on Sunday, I found the place filled with uniformed police toting automatic weapons. Is that normal now?' I asked.

'Sounds like there was a heightened alert of some sort,' he replied.

'You know,' I said 'I came out of the customs area and a young policeman instantly fixed his gaze on me. I went straight to the men's room to wash a bit. When I came out, there he was again, his right hand on the trigger guard, talking to a sergeant and looking at me suspiciously.'

"Well, they are trained to look for anything unusual, out of place, odd, different, too much baggage, too little baggage, walking too fast or too slow and so on,' he said.

How about a latent face, I thought, thinking about Inspector Law just across the river, a long time ago.

It's too bad I couldn't tell Alex then that I had met the same bobby and the same sergeant waiting for me when I got to Heathrow two days later. However, I visited the factory and got all the information to stop the disease at Manchester. Which I did.

I suppose it hadn't been a very profitable visit, considering all factors, but I didn't feel too bad about it all until I got back to London. I had literally forgotten about policemen when I alighted from the taxi at Heathrow for the return trip to Toronto. I was surprised to feel it so hot and humid, compared with Scotland. I had come down by train to see the countryside, quite difficult to do at one hundred miles an hour, with station signs placed parallel to the track for the days of steam and now ashamed to be read. 'ZIP', they all said. *Talking signs*, I thought! I had also asked the taxi driver to take it easy through the back streets of the city so I could peer into the lives of all the Londoners on a Wednesday morning.

All was well and good! So I had forgotten about the police security people.

I had an hour or so to wait and it seemed to be hot even in the airport building, and for some reason I got it into my head that I'll bet the bloody air conditioner is not working on the aircraft and that a six-hour sticky flight lay ahead.

I did not think much of the idea of travelling in comparative discomfort unnecessarily, so I wandered into a trendy airport shop and looked around the shelves – I had no idea what I was looking for – when I noticed the very same policeman looking at me through the window, over some bookshelves.

Just a coincidence, I thought, although I've never believed in them very much; confluence of events perhaps, but coincidence, well, I have a problem there most times.

Forget it, I said to myself, so I bought a cricketing magazine with some hilarious cartoons in it and was reading one when I burst out laughing! It depicted village green cricket and a rather portly batsman getting his head in the way of a new ball in the early afternoon.

The caption was something like, 'The Right Honorable St. John Braithwaite deflecting a bouncer with disdain after a good lunch at the Three Ferrets.'

Well, unfortunately, I had been insulated from cricket for years and I just couldn't help bursting out laughing, gales of it! Unfortunately, I forgot that security people do not like people who laugh while being watched and I was a bit dismayed to see the policeman sort of perk up a bit and mumble into his communication pack. I still tried to take things normally so I looked around and bought a nice box of lavender talcum powder by Yardley. This would be my answer to the anticipated discomfort on the plane. I would go into the men's room and liberally apply talcum powder about everywhere. Seemed like a damned sensible idea at the time. The gales of laughter from me brought the attention of a gentleman next to me at the magazine rack; he was strikingly like the cricketer, but in a blue blazer and gray trousers. God almighty, *FIVE*, I thought! He eyed me up and down for about ten seconds, then saw the short-sleeved buttoned down cotton shirt and tie with lightweight jacket over my arm and briefcase. First he thought I was American, then he glanced at the cricket magazine and changed his mind. His eyes said 'Australian or something'.

Meanwhile, I was heading for the men's room to liberally apply the talcum. Which I did, lots! I walked along to a stand-up bar and ordered a gin and tonic while looking around for the policeman. I couldn't see him, but the airport was crowded. I had my drink and then I did the wrong thing. One end of the room was empty, at the window, so I wandered across and set my briefcase and jacket down to glance at the magazine. Now I could see him about sixty feet away, once again talking into his communicator. I am sure he thought I was going to leave the briefcase by the window and walk away. He had it all figured out by himself. I stooped down to pick up my briefcase and when I stood up he was gone, vanished!

My flight had been announced for departure in about one hour, so I thought that I might as well relax, go upstairs to a second floor bar and have another drink. So with no policeman in sight, I went up the stairs and across to the bar. I thought that he must have evaluated the situation and decided that I was just another traveler behaving in an odd fashion.

I got the drink from the barman and turned to find a table, and just visible on the stairs was the characteristic blue helmet and eyes only of the London bobby watching my every move. I walked across to a table where an American girl was sitting. I said to her, 'Do you mind if I sit here?' again glancing at the helmet which looked as if it was sitting on the floor like an enormous dark blue mouse!

She said, 'Be my guest,' so I sat down on the chair with a thump, misjudging altitude.

Suddenly my shirt sleeves, collar and waist band exploded in a cloud of white dust, accompanied by hoots of laughter from the American girl who was looking at me questioningly. 'Summerdust, ma'am, just summerdust,' I said, glancing at London's finest who, now finally, was laughing, too, and shaking his helmeted head.

Bloody Americans, I thought so!

COOL STUART JIMSON

'Understatement' is a well known trait in the British. Some time ago, while on a visit, an item in a Scottish newspaper caught my attention as the ultimate expression of this fascinating racial idiosyncrasy.

It ran as follows: 'Early yesterday morning, a farmer in the south of Scotland reported to the local constabulary that overnight someone had stolen a two hundred yard length of his five-foot-high stone wall.'

'This is one of our more unusual cases!' said the local police sergeant, crystallizing the trait in good style.

Well sir, or ma'am, if I said I was apprehensive at the thought of my first visit underground in a highly dangerous coal mine many years ago, that comment would leave the above understatement at the post.

Valleyfield, the name of this now happily closed mine, was talked about in hushed tones in those days, since the memory of a terrible explosion underground which had killed many men still lingered in the minds of most, and especially me.

I would say if it had not been for the priceless antics of my guide and mentor, Stuart Jimson, during that first trip underground, I would have proceeded forthwith for the Americas (as I did years later) the very next day.

Most deep underground coal mines, all the world over, look the same: a complex of high steel head-frames, silently spinning wheels above the mine shaft; dust, dirty buildings, often with small paned windows, and the eternal hiss of steam night and day leaking from the labyrinth of insulated overhead pipes, and very few people around. Everyone is deep underground, in the city beneath.

That's how it was when Stuart and I changed into dark coveralls, put on our steel-capped boots, strapped our heavy batteries on our hips and clipped our headlamps onto our hard hats.

All Stuart's gear, of course, was suitably beat up with the wear and tear of the years; however, I felt very conspicuous in my new coveralls, shiny boots and new hard hat. As we walked across the yard, prior to climbing up the point where we were to go into the cage for the descent, I discreetly shuffled up clouds of dust to hopefully coat myself with grime and hence look reasonable for this special occasion.

Well, we approached the filthy and wet steel cage – in actual fact nothing but a big steel box covered with dust, damp and dirt and attached to a two thousand foot long steel string.

Quickly, I remember thinking, a bell rang and somebody did something and we dropped like a stone into the blackness. I tried not to dwell on the fact that the now swallowing hole racing and rattling up under my feet was deeper than the Empire State Building is high.

In a few minutes we reached the bottom of the shaft and the start of a long, long tunnel about twelve feet wide, called the sea mine; seemed like a reasonable name to me, since we were almost two thousand feet or so beneath the salt sea at the time.

We were surveyors, you see, or at least he was supposed to be, and I wanted to learn the business, since I was told *once* that the world was a surveyor's oyster (it is), and if it was a good enough endeavor for a while for George Washington and Abraham Lincoln, it should be good enough for me.

Stuart Jimson was a big man, six feet three inches tall but he had a bad right leg, he limped at all times; and the survey crews always walked underground in Indian file behind him whether two or ten of us, and in order of then current importance.

Now Stuart was more of a character than a surveyor. I observed even then that there were a lot more surveyors than there were characters in the world, and I realized you can learn a lot more about life in the presence of one of the former category than you can with the latter.

I guess that we firmly established his sense of humor and mine as we walked in the long sea mine, which was actually two miles long, but shadowing Stuart, it seemed closer to four miles.

Stuart would appear to have been having trouble with his old and antique car, and he said after walking in darkness and silence for ages, 'You know, I can't get a new front axle for my car for love nor money.' It seemed somehow inappropriate for me to reply in the silence that built up down there; so we shuffled on for about thirty seconds and he turned his head as he walked, blinding me with the white glare of the lamp on his head, and said with a twinkle in his eye, 'Come to think of it – I haven't tried money!'

I could see that he and I would get along well, and I saw there and then that the only way to survive really in mines or other such tough places was to cultivate some sense of humor...

We walked on and he complained every now and again about his bad leg, but it must have been with tongue in cheek because I don't remember feeling too sorry for him.

Eventually we reached the coal face, which was as black as a crow's belly, a steeply inclined hole in the coal about eight feet high, hot and deserted since this was not a bustling coal shovelin' production shift.

He announced with due ceremony and dramatically, 'We are now going up the coal face!' I truthfully felt like disputing that statement, but in mines or other places very nasty things happen to people not caught up in the enthusiasm of such moments; 'Fine with me, Stuart! Lead on,' I said as a precaution, just in case he had any ideas about me going first.

We had gone about one hundred long, steep and exhausting yards, and I was covered with dust and sweat, panting away behind Stuart who was ten feet ahead of me and struggling up the rough slippery grade, now genuinely cursing his bad leg.

Suddenly, on our right hand side, there was a god-awful and very loud breaking and crushing noise – we both turned our heads to the right in a split second, to see massive coal the size of a boxcar preparing to topple over on us and snuff us both right there and then.

Well, in the heat of the moment I thought this was a bit much on my maiden voyage underground, but I moved much faster then, than I have ever moved before or since, toward a safety niche twenty feet to my left. I didn't pause for a millisecond to think about poor (lame?) Stuart, and I was at the safe ground in no more than two seconds flat as the massive coal tumbled and shattered against my heels in clouds of dust, fragmenting against my back and shoulders.

Well, when I flashed into the niche, there he was, already comfortably seated in residence, eyes twinkling red, as they do underground, through a black dusty face with white teeth sparkling, and grinning from ear to ear.

'What kept you, laddie?' said cool Stuart Jimson.

THE SOUTHERN PRINCESS

'I could take you and by surprise any time,' she seemed to say. Her breathtaking beauty and her blue and white swirling dress deceived me when I first saw her. Quite full of mischief and promises to be spoiled had to be her plan.

Dreamlike, no doubt about that, now here, now there, elusive, a taunt or tease of some kind perhaps to get my attention.

'I am a seachild,' she said to me in a whisper. 'I do have a name you will remember, but you can call me 'Oh' for now.'

I did not see her again for some time after the first encounter and it did not bother me one bit. Oh, I thought about her to be sure. Quite unapproachable, with exotic origins. Any moves to be made would be hers. She alone would choose, not me, I hope. Why bother anyway. She was now several thousand miles away and I was not, so she cannot find me here or there. But unlikely meetings do take place in Louisiana and that's what really bothered me now. It really is scary here. I probably should move again to the north, where I feel better. Away from swamp and sea, that has to be the idea. Yes. Yes. I would be safe if I was away from the sea, far to the north.

'I can take you by surprise any time,' she said. I wish she hadn't, but I bet she knew exactly what she was doing when she pinned her dark shadow on me at the start.

I don't think that I would have been so afraid if I hadn't noticed her right hand, almost hidden in her cotton dress, when I first saw her. I remember thinking that it looks as though she was grasping an invisible orange.

Oh, hell, this is much, much better warm inside and getting cold outside. A long way from those sweaty sea things, none of them very nice for very long.

Yes, this really is better and safer, too; probably be able to sleep here, I would think after all of those other places. So many of them strange.

I wonder where she is, how close could she be?

Never mind, there is no reason at all for her to follow seven thousand miles across two continents for revenge. It just doesn't make either sense or nonsense. It's just not possible.

So she did leave Louisiana some days ago, so what, but that's not good, that's not good at all.

Those long damned searching fingers, you knew they would be a problem. God, what on earth is that noise?

It just can't be what I think it is, not here.

It just can't be, not away up here.

Not me... not my house... not now.

Opal, not now... not any time.

THE MANDATE OF GAZPACHO

'Preposterous!'

'What did you say, Gassy?'

'I said preposterous, dangerous and ridiculous! And perhaps anomalous, too! We will see.'

'Are these wild animals or what, then, Gassy?'

'No, stupid, they're adjectives!'

'If you choose English as your principal language, you are expected to understand it and speak it reasonably well, you know.'

'One reason why I call myself Gazpacho.'

'Well, all right, then, what is "preposterous, dangerous, ridiculous and perhaps anomalous, too" Gazpacho?'

'Just about everything, really, come to think of it, but I was referring to these people, as they say, down there where you're going again.'

'On earth?'

'They don't seem to have learned much at all, through all those years, as they call them. Absolutely ignorant, totally, of the concept of scale and insignificance! Mars for God's sake!!'

'But there you have it.'

'Even with all our people down there, too, for who knows how long now.'

'Still, I suppose it's none of my business, really. Not my problem. Briefing and exit intelligence is my game. Some say my mandate.'

'You seen the Quartermonster yet and got all you need?'

'Yes, Gassy, I've got it all; not much needed down there, it would seem.'

'Why can't we take some of our new things? Help a lot, I would think.'

'Sorry, just not allowed, not for a long time, anyway.'

'Why on earth do we keep going there, I always ask. Still, it will be interesting to see if biology has a use for them.' 'There, on Earth, I mean! Earth! That's a good one, Earth. Eh, Stupid! It's inaccurate, silly and doesn't even sound right.' 'But there you have it; sounds vulgar, too. Earth! Ugh! They even gave all of us a better name. Andromeda! Galaxy too, no less. Their best known constellation.'

'Andromeda, Gassy? Where did they get that name?'

'Oh, Greeks, I suppose; they're always pinching names from them, that's the lot we sent down some time ago; promising but they sort of fizzled out.'

'Clever people, too!'

'Look here, come to think of it, I can't keep calling you stupid! It's... well... a sort of an implied insult. We can't have that, can we?'

'How about we call you Gene? Sounds good, doesn't it?'

'That's it! Gene, you are, a bit like my name and short for Gazogene! Unique. Named after an early portable device for making flavored, ahem, soda water. Device wasn't really a success, though. It was laughed out of existence by Scottish schoolboys many years ago. You see, during the process a rather rude expulsion of gas was required and they all spilled their drinks while laughing at it all! Those were the days, too.'

'Gazogene the First sounds good; Gene for short!'

'Well, if you say so, Gassy. It sounds good to me, too!'

'Well, Gene, what was I saying before we found you a name? Oh, yes, something about fizzling out! Good phrase there, Gene, fizzling out as, say, opposed to fizzling in. Two simple expressions I stole from that, er, English, what, language to encompass all unknown Extra Terrestrial Galactic Submolecular Illogical Systems.'

'This includes us here, Gene, in the Andromeda, in case you are not quite following me yet. No matter! Ho ho ho! That's one of my stellar jokes, get it, Gene? Never was, eh? Matter, that is!'

'I get it, Gassy, molecularly always very quick you were.'

'You know, Gene, now that we're passing the time of day, so to speak, while we're getting things ready.'

'We picked up their sense of humor down there only relatively recently; very interesting, I might say. We found that it's the best sense they have! At least in the European theatre of our cultural analysis!'

'That's where I really specialize.'

'Indeed.'

'Yes.'

'That's why they call me Gazpacho in the front office!'

'Since Andromeda is, or was, or will be awash in a cold, hot, entropic and galactically colorful soup.'

'This arrangement is best, for now, analogized by European Gaspacho!'

'Best described as an attractive dish of Italian tomatoes; love them! Coolish cucumbers from England! Red Spanish peppers and, of course, what else, onions from France. *formidable!*'

'And best served in summer, right, Gassy?'

'Absolutely right there, Gene!'

'You're catching on, Boyo!'

'Piping up, when required!'

'As I was saying about picking up their sense of humor!'

'Well, that's all true, Gene.'

'It used to be a yawn here.'

'We didn't have anything to laugh at until we accidentally, er, tapped into their, er, space radio signals.'

'Remember those, Gene?'

'Do so, Gassy!'

'They've sent a few, you know, Gene, and we got them all!'

'The very first were in Horse Code, all dots and dashes and stuff.'

'Negative Enn Primitive Classification, of course.'

'Well that was the long and the short of it anyway.'

'Did you get it again, Gene?'

'A bit of a laugh!'

'Yes, Gassy, I got it again, very impressive, I must say!'

'Well, anyway, Gene, about these messages, sort of wandering space buoys in the Galactic Sea, all looking for the fisherman, I would surmise?'

'Well, we got the first one, and let it go by, then the second; we let that go by, too. Interesting stuff on that one. Pity.'

'But the third he handled quite differently!'

'By then, we had caught on to their ways of doing things; through ReEntry Intelligence, mainly and the signal compositions themselves, you might say. We had their number! As they would say, or so we thought!'

'Exit strategy, my division, we, I say we; were asked by the front office to send a reply! Not only, I say, send it, but we were asked to compose it! To be compiled with the intrinsic soul of brevity was my only directive! To wit; wit! As they say.'

'Well, Gassy, what was the actual message then?'

'Oh, right simple, Gene, ridiculously simple, I thought, but alas, too simple for them.'

'We sent the single word, "a–n–d", just following the receipt of their signal. Rather clever, I thought, "a–n–d", to let you understand, Gene; this was first to identify ANDROMEDA, secondly to let them know we understood their conditional way of most propositions, meaning that there's always an "and" with them, and thirdly that we appreciated, by that comment, their wonderful sense of humor!'

'Well, Gazpacho, what can I say? But what did they say?'

'Well, Gene, old man, they got it but they didn't get it! In one ear and out the other, into primordial space. Just haven't evolved into the single ear species yet!'

'How come then, Gassy?'

'Gene, if you can believe it, it was one for the black book! Stupid sods! Preposterous, I said at the time. They thought the signal was "Do not acknowledge." They totally missed the identification facet of the signal; hadn't a bloody clue it was related to our understanding of them and their sense of humor, too. Dangerous and ridiculous, I felt they were, at the time! Fumblers!'

'Well, what really happened, Gassy, do you think?'

'Oh, I know what happened, all right, Gene, *I* know what happened!'

'Well, Gene?'

'It seems two geezers at the University of Calgary were playing chess when our signal came zapping in! We sent in a triple burst signal ten program a–n–d–! a–n–d–! a–n–, that is. We repeated the burst ten times, each burst spaced in a progression, so they would recognize structure.'

'Good thinking. What happened then, Gassy?'

'Well, Gene, our people down there tell us that there was a bit of a stampede in Calgary, with chess pieces flying all over the place in the ensuing confusion, you see, while their receiver was open, their recording device was not, so they had to scramble to find a pad and a pencil! Wouldn't you know it! Anderson three – that's our operative down there – got a copy of the pad and the received signal. Inthelightofallthe-moonsinthesky it said, "D–n–a–, d–n–a–, d–n–a"!'

'What happened then, Gassy? It's the wrong way round. A farce backwards, I think, is their expression, Gazogene old chap.'

'It seems that they transposed the signal in the reception oriented modem; called their American friends immediately; made a one eighty about turn in their studies of molecular structures and heredity and never even had the good manners to tell anybody that we got their message!'

'Well Gassy, do you want me to straighten them out?'

'No Gene, don't bother; too late now, anyway; they're off and running with all their "D–N–A" stuff now.'

'Surprises there for them, too, I'll bet! Relatively speaking. Well, Gene, to be serious about your exit now. You about ready?'

'Am so, Gassy. Delivery system still the same?'

''Fraid so, Gene. Oh, one more thing, Gene; our people.'

'Down there?'

'Most all begin with a... n... d, people and places too! You know, Andrew, Andropov, Anderson and so forth! Places too, remember! Andros, Andover, etc., Andelusia, Samarkand too!'

'Oh Samarkand, those were the days, wow!'

'Hot days and cool nights! Ah!'

'Yes, I use to have a real good carpet business going there for a while; sort of disappeared by itself you might say, just floated off! Yes, I was going to call the business Tamerlane's Carpet Emporium. Unfortunately the local people took offense. Had to call it Samarkanderson Rugs! Specialized in floor to air pieces! A bit of all right that was, Gazogene me old China!'

'Patching you into the system now. Won't take a moment.'

'Gene is for Go.'

'Catch them as they fly, old man!

'Moments, that is!'

THE CHEESE CLIMBER

'Just nobody could possibly climb away up here!' said Fraser to his wife. 'It's impossible.'

'Well, unless he's got wings or something,' she added and continued, 'we haven't seen too many angels around here for some time, good ones. Not for a long time,' she said, sweeping her eyes from the mountains to the north and round to the Moray Firth, shrouded white by a cold mist, like a pillow to a red sunrise.

'Anyway, it's just too cold to talk away up here,' she said gathering her woolens around her and gazing down the wet side of the mossy green tower to her dogs barking at the door far below her feet.

'Besides, Roderick,' she said, 'it's only a cheese.'

'It's not only a cheese at all this time,' he said quietly, scratching the side of his red beard. 'It's more than that, I think.' He continued, 'It's always more than that, and the dogs didn't bark; strange, this is the third cheese in two months; two from the table in the Creamerie Barn and now this one, from the top of a stone tower one hundred feet high. When Fairbairn built this tower, it was for defense and safety; it was built with stones and mortar all angled and set, so no man could climb his tower; strange!'

'Well,' his wife said, 'somebody did; the oak and iron door was still locked and we found the cheese gone.'

He looked at her and said, 'It can't be climbed by any man, I told you, there's no iron spikes or slits until eighty feet above the ground and new spikes won't hold in the angles of the stones and crumbly soft mortar. It was designed so a man's weight, moving, would pull out the spikes,' he added.

'Well, there's a lot of stranger things have happened around here, without being able to be explained,' she retorted.

'True enough,' said Fraser. 'But these things were unexplainable, which is really an explanation in itself, for a while at least,' he added, his mind drifting like a boat.

'It's no angel; I'll agree with you there.' he said. 'This looks to me like mischief, not thieving,' he said as he continued his reasoning. 'It feels like someone is challenging me, almost, to solve the problem.'

Fairbairn had clearly said, 'No man can possibly climb his tower.'

'Well, now? Well, now?'

'Then what about a boy, a wee boy with a big heart and strong fingers and toes,' he mused, smiling. 'A wee boy, then, who thinks like a lion and moves like a spider. Aye, up the wall, in the cracks wi' hardly any weight at all! Just like a spider; or even two spiders.' he added. 'If it's who I think it might be, the fair challenge and the cheese and a puzzle, too, for me would suit him right down to the ground.'

'How long has Roderick been at his old mountain mischievous grannies then? Tell me that? And I'll solve the problem!'

'Get yir boots out of my face. Fir God's sake.'

'Man it's difficult enough, Rory, without you slippin' and slidin' like that; good God you're makin' enough noise to waken them all up! Besides you're supposed to be good at this! As far as I'm concerned you couldnae climb up to Jessie Miller's windae wi a ladder. Aye, and she sleeps on the first floor, tae!'

'Ian, you be quiet, will you? Besides, I've never climbed this place before, what do you bloody well expect? It's green, wet and slippery.'

Rory continued, looking down at his companion, 'Anyway I told you to stay at the bottom; I don't like to talk when, well, I'm going up in the world.'

'Aye, Rory, that will be right, but if you keep slippin' like that you'll be back doon soon enough! Just you mind to tell me before you try out your wings!'

'I'll do that, Ian. Which language would you like the message in?'

'Gaelic, French or English.'

'Hush now, Ian, lad.'

'Hold on tight now; I think we're up!'

'Well, now, would you look at that?'

'That wa' will take some dingin' doon!'

'Tie the long rope to the three iron spikes and throw the coils down, quickly.'

'Make sure it's secure, and you go back down and tie it in here and there, you know what to do! Mind you don't fall! I'll just have a wee quiet look at the bonnie view up here, before the sun comes up, and other things, too. Hey, Ian, if ye see himself, tell him I'm going to look for my breakfast!'

'Rory, you stay there till I make sure all is well. You stay there!'

'It's probably all the wine and the cheese,' the soldier said.

'What did you say, Major?' his thoughts broken.

'I said, sir, that it's probably all the wine and the cheese why they're are all so quiet up there.'

'Perhaps so, Major, but it's more than that. It's quiet because it's night, and it's quiet because we've been here for some time now and it's also quiet because they don't know what's going to happen next, nor when, where or how. Their advantage is the fortress, our advantage is not known to them as yet. They feel that we cannot surprise them for our ships have been here for days, remember. This is a far different affair than on the Moray Firth thirteen years ago when I was about your age, Major, and a young officer, too. The cannon there spelled death for clans and cause. Here, the long cannon says *"mettre en garde"* perhaps; as the ships drift back and forth, back and forth with the tide! Left to right, right to left. Beware, I say to him, in my silence, for I am at your door, now.'

'General, I can see that, the seemingly silent deserted ships swinging as a fleet, chained on the end of a long pendulum, imaginary, of course, night and day must dull and confuse the Gallic senses.'

'You know that may be true, Major, perhaps someone should look into that proposition.'

'I try to think like him up there, Andrew. Not like me for now, besides.'

'Perhaps he thinks we are in no hurry to die?'

'Maybe so, sir, but perhaps he thinks also that we are in an impossible position to attack.'

'Major, he knows this position can be attacked and he knows how; that is, the usual diversions here and there and then frontal assault. To the fortress; well, he's right, Major, dead right.'

'General, the rocks are far worse than Edinburgh; did you know that, sir, before we came?'

'Yes, Andrew, I did know that and I came prepared. Major, would you kindly ask Captain Fraser if he would come to my cabin as soon as possible now, and would you please come with him? I am now in need of his services, please tell him.'

'Yes, Captain Fraser, I know this is not the route up the cliff which we discussed and I also know it's the most difficult place on the entire escarpment; that's why I want to go up that way. Besides our people tell me that no one has ever climbed up that part of the cliff.'

'I ask, can you do it, Mr. Fraser?'

'Well, General, I can't do it, but I know who can. I know who can, sir. The kinsman I have in mind is small enough not to be seen, brave enough to try, daft enough to think he can do it and also hungry enough to succeed! All I have to do, General, is tell him that they keep their cheese behind the stone *Poudriere* and that way up is the only one unguarded! All we have to do, then, is follow him to the trap before it springs! General Wolfe.'

'Ah, shall we go to Quebec City, then, gentlemen?'

'That we shall, General, that we shall.'

'Quiet as a mouse then Mr. Fraser, *s'il vous plait.*'

'Would you look at that now, the Citadel at Quebec!'

'Just think!'

'Just after sunrise in 1759, what a sight!'

'Two thousand men died here in twenty minutes!' said the guide; driving the *caleche* and reining his horse as quietly as possible over the cobblestone street.

'It's difficult to forget, even now,' he continued. 'Both generals died here on the Heights of Abraham, and waited to keep their appointments, too!' he said as if it were yesterday, pointing to the green and treed parkland stretching away to the cliffs and river beyond and away below.

'*Je me souvien,* that's what they say here; but this place is what I think they mean, I will remember!'

'I still often wonder,' the guide said. 'how an army ever got into position at this fortress. *La sourciére pour les Anglais.* That's what they thought. It must have been the cheese, that's it, somebody smelled the cheese! *Quel qu'un!*'

'Qui.'

WEST OF GREENWICH WON'T DO

'Out where the skies are a little bit bluer, out where the hearts are a little bit truer, that's where the West begins!'

So goes, more or less, a well known Canadian verse, in an almost spiritual answer to the question often asked in Canada, 'Where does the West begin?'

The 'West' is much different from the 'East'; everybody knows this reality. It's not the same. People and places are quite different. However this question has never really been answered satisfactorily. Does it start in Manitoba, or maybe Saskatchewan? This might make sense; they don't call themselves 'Easterners'. So by, well, 'logical reasoning' the Manitoba and Ontario border must be the changeover from an Easterner to a Westerner? But for some reason nobody buys this idea, it's too simple and just does not feel right. When a dilemma such as this arises, it's usually because people are going about looking for the right solution the wrong way. A common error.

I seem to be the only one who has it right, I think!

The Canadian West starts in Calgary, Alberta, and by emanation, that is a cultural 'backburn', it goes to the East and towards the Atlantic and goes West to the far West and the Pacific. The West stops at the Pacific; that is definite, because then we have the Far East.

Really the West is a North–South thing, a vertical concept. The core of the North American West follows the trails of the cattle drives between Texas and Alberta. Then the emanation takes place; both East and West, the Americans go East to their MidWest, but Canadians go East to the East, but do not know where it starts.

Hence the problem and question.

Let's see if we can figure it out, since this is a short story; we will have to go by plane from Calgary to Toronto, as I did a few years ago, following a train journey through the Rocky Mountains from Vancouver to Calgary.

So, let's go flying!

The silver-podded plane was spiraling upwards almost lazily into the early morning skies of Alberta. There the skies really are bluer, it would seem, and without clouds from horizon to horizon that morning.

The Selkirk range of mountains in British Columbia falls behind the massive tailplane as the red glint of the early morning sun shines on the South Saskatchewan River as it appears over the wings. As we climbed to cruising altitude, I was thinking about the train journey through about four hundred miles of towering mountains. The journey in itself was spectacular, but I particularly wanted to see the Rogers Pass through the Selkirk range, since an engineering friend of mine had designed and built special steel tunnels for avalanche protection for the railroad. I did see these structures, which were built to withstand snow fifty feet deep, crossing them at two hundred miles per hour. Quite a feat and very imaginatively designed for safe travel.

This was a Canadian first!

I was thinking about this when I noticed the soft Scottish accent of my traveling companion-to-be. My mind started to change gear a little, and I could see that although he was a bit younger he must have been born within twenty miles of my own birthplace. I said nothing at first. My mind shifted to how I could tell him that I had a bunch of kippers hanging outside my twelfth floor hotel room in Calgary. This was a present from a friend from Newfoundland who had attended a meeting with me at Banff on the Alberta side, just, of the Rocky Mountains.

I never did tell him about the kippers.

He had heard my accent, too, as I spoke to the flight attendant, and as the plane banked with the city of Calgary disappearing, 'Just a pile of rocks, Jock!' he said, in a typically direct Scottish manner; easily misunderstood by some.

'I suppose it is,' I said, taking a last look at the disappearing city. 'The people are very friendly, though,' I said, softening his opening gambit.

'James is my name,' he said. 'James Keddie,' he added, pushing a polished paw across, un-jeweled, from a well cut blazer sleeve.

'You're from Edinburgh, aren't you?' he confidently continued.

'No,' I said, 'but close.' I added, 'Some schooling there, though; cricket, too. Are you?' I asked. 'From Edinburgh, I mean.'

'Yes,' he replied, 'from Corstorphine, actually.'

'Oh,' I responded, 'I have three cousins there. All girls.'

'Really,' said James, noting the situation but not responding.

So now taking the conversational offensive, I said, at point blank range, 'James, you must be a marketing manager.'

'How the hell did you know that?' he jabbed back, twisting in his seat.

'I am of the same ilk, nowadays,' I replied. 'Steel,' I added, in the manner Bond. 'You?'

'Wine,' he said, quickly trumping my card, with some *élan*.

'Oh, good. Charles is my name,' I said, 'late of Dunfermline toun.'

'So what were you doing in Calgary?' he said, opening up the conversation.

'Nothing,' I said.

'Me, too,' he crisply countered without explanation.

I was actually returning from a meeting in Victoria on Vancouver Island and I told him so, and also about my train trip through the Rocky Mountains.

Soon he said and predictably, at cruising altitude, 'I wonder if they have any of our wine on board?'

'Pity that you don't carry a line of Scotch whisky!' I said, escalating the situation.

'Bombay gin all right?' he said, smiling and again turning his seat.

'Make mine large and with limes!' I said, ignoring the morning sun and everything else.

'Good man,' he replied. 'Two large gins, Bombay, please, ice and limes,' he said to the amused attendant, correctly evaluating the situation.

'Live ones!' she thought!

'Well it sure beats black flies and a canoe as our Scottish ancestors endured to explore this country,' he said, passing me the nice cool glass and settling back a bit.

'Yes, it does,' I said. 'We owe them a lot, I think.'

'*Slainte!*' he said with a dab of Gaelic, while raising his glass to acknowledge them.

'Fort Macleod and Mackenzie! I responded, being more specific and colorful.

'What brought you to Canada?' he said, after a pause.

'Well, for a wandering Scot, then in the mining business, the East did not make sense twenty years ago, it was too hot and basically too troubled then.'

'I thought the very same, you know,' he replied. 'Hey ho to the Americas and all that!' he added. 'Worked out pretty good, too, so far. But you know some of us must have gone east; I wonder how they got along.'

'Yes, I know of one who did all right,' I said. 'Name of Rintoul, worked for the international division of our company in Singapore. Bit of a laugh with him, James. It seems that the National Geographic took a casual picture of the Long Bar in the Raffles hotel and Rintoul knew the first names of every person sitting at the bar! That was in the sixties,' I added.

'Well,' he said, 'you know what they say about the sixties in Canada. If you can remember them, you weren't there! Same in Singapore, I guess.'

'I suppose so,' I said, glancing out the window to my left and warming up to the conversation. 'There's the movable city! Not Paris.'

'What do you mean by that?' he said, trying to see out the window.

'Oh, I mean Regina,' I replied. 'I once made a trip at night in a car from the west and I asked my associate what was the glow on the horizon. "Regina," he said. "Regina, Saskatchewan!" he added. About sixty miles away, the prairies are pretty flat, you know. Well, James, we drove for two hours and the glow was still on the horizon.'

'I guess this country is so big they can afford to move their towns overnight,' he laughed as we cruised at five hundred miles an hour towards Manitoba.

I was now quite intrigued by the panorama on such a clear morning, so I said to him, looking down again, 'You see that big snake down there? That's the Qu'appelle river valley.'

'A great uncle of mine came out here many years ago and built a log cabin at Tantallon, I've seen it!'

'I bet he knew where the West begins!' I added sort of innocently, Henry Hamilton did.

'Oh, yes,' said James, 'the eternal question in Canada, you mean?'

'Yes,' I replied. 'By the way, do you happen to know?'

'Where the West begins, you mean? Matter of fact, I do, old chap,' he responded. 'It starts when the time changes! Fleming's idea and all that! When Eastern Standard time stops.'

'Well, how bloody clever of you!' I replied, turning in my seat belt. 'I never thought of it that way,' I said, just a bit miffed at being upstaged so easily. He knew that he had scored a point!

'Five hours west of Greenwich, Mean Time,' he added, rubbing salt in the wound.

'Greenwich! Herstmonceux, to be correct,' I said, in retaliation.

'What's that?' questioned James.

'The observatory was at Herstmonceux,' I said, trying to regain some measure of comfort. 'Anyway,' I continued to retaliate, 'Where does Eastern Standard Time stop? On the ground, I mean.'

'Where the west begins, I dare say.'

'By the way, was one of your cousins called Catherine?'

THE FOUR HOLER

Not so long ago, my family of three and I were asked to look after a large farmhouse near Toronto for a period of six months while the owners were in Europe. The farm had been originally about two hundred acres but was now considerably less. The area was and still is very fashionable for some of our more well-to-do country dwellers and city workers.

The house itself, built in the early years of the nineteenth century, had been modernized in every way without losing its basic charm. It was elegantly furnished and finished throughout, but seemed to have an overload of bathrooms.

Four, to be exact, in a house which originally had none.

Now one of the many extraordinary things that we found out living in the place was that people can very readily adapt to a surplus of bathrooms and before long all of them were in regular use, so to speak, and the whole experience had added a new dimension to our lives. However, it also brought about some personal complexity since a decision, or several directional decisions, were required to deal with each natural urge.

Anyway, before too long, we hadn't the faintest notion how we would possibly get along without the four bathrooms; they became part of our way of life in that rambling old country house.

Now since I had lived in towns and cities most of my life, I had never given a great deal of thought as to where water came from before it emerged sparkling from the tap, nor was I curious about it either because it didn't seem relevant.

However, a rude awakening and enlightenment was in store for me as I was introduced to the peculiarities of a dug well. An old dug well.

You see, one day the water stopped coming out of the taps and also, to my consternation, stopped filling the cisterns of our now indispensable four bathrooms. It didn't take me too long to figure out that there must be something far wrong here and, after poking around a bit at the well and looking at the rusty connecting pipes, pump and valves in the cellar, without results, decided I had better call somebody in town.

To tackle this water problem a plumber seemed like the closest sense to me; so he duly arrived and swanned around inspecting the well, which was covered with a patio, complete with picnic table, all about to fall into a great hole!

'The pump is broken, the well is caving in and the pipes are also corroded,' he announced, after about an hour, 'and it will take about four days to fix and it will cost you nineteen hundred dollars.' Just like that!

Anyway, the real implication of this statement was slowly sinking in: no water; and we were stuck with four orphaned bathrooms for four days!

Well, I soon solved the problem; drinking water could come in containers from the spring near the village, and the cisterns in the bathrooms could be easily filled by taking up buckets of water from the water-laden swimming pool!

I thought this was pretty heady thinkin' and stuff, and had the attractive quality of simplicity, so the routines were established to service the four bathrooms.

The actual technique was also simple; we put a plastic bucket on a twenty-foot length of rope, then heaved it into the pool and lugged the dripping bucket indoors and filled up the cisterns. Strange though it may seem looking back, it never once occurred to any of us that we only needed to use one bathroom!

Anyway, one summer Saturday morning I recall being engaged in the pail-slinging part of the operation at the pool, when I looked upwards to see an Air Canada jet making a nose-up approach to the airport. Having looked at the pools in many places from up there more than just a few times myself coming back late, I visualized some ambitious young and tired businessman looking aimlessly at the countryside slipping by below and spotting this beautiful spread with me slinging a bucket into the pool.

If his thoughts were directed to figuring out how could a fellow smart enough to own a big place like that still be stupid enough to empty his swimming pool with a bucket, I would not have been at all surprised.

BOOMER PATRICK'S FANCY CAR

Cape Tormentine and Baie Chaleur on the wild Atlantic coastline with Quebec to the north. The great tidal basin of Fundy and the seaport of Saint John to the south. The US state of Maine to the west; all encircle and capture New Brunswick. The mighty and beautiful Saint John river wide for most of the way down the west side of this Canadian province, is a dominant feature and was, in the past, the main transportation system for people and products, through the extensive forests of this part of Canada. Today, you can see massive forest products plants looking like futuristic islands in a sea of coniferous trees from horizon to horizon. Transportation today is by gleaming monster trucks on long hauls to the housing markets of Ontario, and particularly to the US south where the demand for Canadian cedar and pine seems endless.

This part of the country was included in seventeenth century Acadia, a place of rural peace, after Verrazano and then a French colony for some time. The descendants of the Acadians are still there in spirit, language and culture.

The capital of New Brunswick is Fredericton, while the industrial, communications and transportation center is Moncton, lying to the east.

Moncton has something in common with the city of Sudbury in Ontario, which is a large mining and smelting town. While the people of Sudbury have been accused of making their own clouds it could be said that Moncton folks make their own snow, and lots of it.

I know about that, and it was fun, too!

The fact that geography, culture, cuisine and gastronomy are closely linked is often evident along the valley of the clear Saint John river. Related to bush camps, there we find Country Kitchens now for travelers, with buffet tables, heavily laden with local delicacies in the hands of very hospitable people. An individual must be hard indeed to please, if they do not like fresh bread, a big pot of beans baked in smoked maple syrup, into which has been placed a mustard-coated partridge! This, served with tender fiddlehead ferns, gathered after the spring flooding of the Saint John river, all peppered and buttered New Brunswick style, would please any palate. No wine here, but excellent country ale from a famous local brewery, Moosehead Beer. Their justified motto is to the point: 'Head and Antlers above the rest!'

Such is part of the nature of today's New Brunswick, which spawns characters of some note also, such as my friend Boomer Patrick, engineer, contractor, descendant of Celtic seafarin' men and general all-round hell raiser upon occasion. Tougher than moose hide and softer than a caterpillar's coat fits him, and if he had a big bushy tail he would be easily mistaken for a fox of sorts.

Sometimes. Sometimes not.

Such as the time he was too hasty, to his embarrassment and expense.

Boomer's *faux pas* started innocently enough. Behind Plaster Rock and Renous, in wild country of the upper reaches of the Miramichi River, the Mi'kmaq Indian roamed not so long ago. Some are still there and the French, too.

Today it is a forest one hundred miles square and harvested by small and large companies, with mills to build and mines to sink and work to be obtained by enterprising folks, a bit like Boomer Patrick, who lives one hundred miles away to the south.

If a Forest Products plant has to be expanded, contractors are asked to price the job formally, to the strictest specifications. The successful bidder, usually the lowest, gets the job and a living for himself, his family and many others, too. There is a certain nobility of purpose in such a vocation since he supports, almost directly, other families' needs. His successes or failures are well known soon, as so much can depend on his actions in this land where the work does grow on trees, but not easily or often. So when Boomer blows it, everybody knows it, and sometimes he does just that.

One day, in the spring, when all hopes after the hostile winter are high, an international paper company let it be known that they intended to expand their facilities and that a contract for about two million dollars would be awarded to the successful contractor in the bidding process. This would be one year's work for a small company such as Boomer's, so relative security for some in a precarious world, and Boomer Patrick was an expert in such work. He was given a month to prepare his bid and all that it entailed, but it was not enough.

Despite that amount of time, on the day he was to personally deliver his documents, he realized he was behind final schedule for the three o'clock absolute and final deadline for bid submission. He had his price determined and checked; he had his detailed documents completed and he also had his bid bond from his bank to assure financial stability as required by the company's procedures. His price was $1,830,000. He had a one hundred mile drive to make but he also had his pride and joy to get him there in time. Namely a big black powerful Oldsmobile, a fancy car by most standards and only just delivered a few weeks before.

With the documents on the seat right beside him, he started out to eat up the miles to his destination and hopefully arrive on time, which he did, and just; that is, with ten minutes to spare, no more. Not much, but enough, he thought. He knew the place well, so he parked his car close to the office and grabbed his documents put there in the envelope, and dashed to the front door.

But!

Then he remembered.

That he had left the vital bid bond in his car. Time was close and he sprinted to the car, and then turned ashen white, to the amusement of some French Canadian (ex)-Acadian workers close by. The car was locked, and his keys were in full view on the front seat, along with his precious and essential bid bond! Never one for loss of words or ever failing to make a decision, he shouted to the onlookers, '*Vite! Battoche, Battre, battoche, vite, vite!*' scraping the bottom of his barrel of local French! One of the workers immediately saw his intent and handed him a heavy and handy twenty-eight pound hammer. Boomer smashed the window of his new car, to the amusement of the gathering crowd. He threw down the hammer, grabbed the bid bond and dashed to the office at three o'clock plus two minutes. Late and sadly so, just in time to hear the announcement.

'The low bidder and contractor, subject to review, has come in at one million, seven hundred and twenty-five thousand dollars!'

Decimated. At that announcement, Boomer looked for all the world like a traffic light, as he changed color and as he realized he would have lost anyway, his price was too high. His rage, his rush and the desperate, forever violation of his beautiful new car were all for nothing!

Boomer Patrick was halfway home before he had cooled off, literally, in the open car and settled down a bit, consoling himself with the thought that one year ago he had won, well, a three million dollar contract from these people, made money, and, well, that's how he got his fancy car!

THE STONE BATH

No ghostly whisper then; but still the unearthly sound of mist-cooled engines down the glen. Swoosh!

For a few seconds, a steel gray arrow flushing other birds to flight.

Navy pilots in perfect formation.

'Mind the fire,' said a voice from the green Land Rover.

'Aye, right,' I responded, dropping away back in my mind's vocabulary, for the correct answer here.

'Damn near blew my bloody fire out, too!' I muttered to myself, nursing the nest-like dry moss, twigs and birch back to life, to flare up brightly once again, as does hope with the new day.

It was over twenty years since I had spent the night in a tent in the Scottish Highlands, the last time in the Lairig Ghru near Glen Derry and Braemar. This time just off Rannoch Moor and into Glen Etive under the shadow of Buachaille Etive Mor and Stob Dearg, and handy to the Kingshouse and Glencoe.

All Robert's idea and a good one, and one I will never forget, for more than one reason. I was a long way from Toronto and he felt that was a good thing.

Since he was well aware of my feeling that men of the deep coal are not to be found on the north buttress, we should just relax, enjoy ourselves and do a little fishing. Also enjoy the hospitality of the Kingshouse, which we did, and excellent it was, too!

After setting up a campsite the previous afternoon, we had gone across to the hotel for dinner and talk with some of the guests and several 'lads o' pairts', a bit like myself. It was very enjoyable and a really nice change of pace for me, from North American commercial life. After dinner, and as a finishing touch, the proprietor suggested we join the guests and hotel staff at a bonfire on the moor near the hotel in the pitch black; perhaps onetime witches and warlocks in the glen?

Twenty or thirty people from all over the world was a fitting sight, reflecting the blaze of the fire in their happy faces while nibbling on spicy sausage and good India Pale Ale. After the bonfire fell away to a memory for most, we were in very good shape as we walked the mile or two back to our tent, despite falling in the marsh and walking into a tree or two. All perfectly sensible then, in Scotland.

We more or less fell into our sleeping bags and closed the tent flaps, the wind was rising quickly from the east and it was carrying rain from the North Sea beyond. About ten seconds later, it just seemed, I woke up and it was dawn. The wind was battling the tent and first light was filtering down the glen through clearing skies, now refreshing and cool.

I lay in my sleeping bag reflecting on a few things and also on what I should do next. It's important. I really did not have a choice, after the idea occurred to me.

I wonder if I could light a fire in a windstorm after all these years, I said to myself. I convinced myself I could. *All it takes is good planning*, I thought. *A fire has to be built, constructed that is. Managed. Timed. Ignition by stages, wind protection and all that.*

I went through a whole checklist in my mind; I also thought about forgetting about the whole idea for a while, but finally said to myself, *Let's do it, dammit, let's do it! First time!*

So I did, as usual.

I think I had passed Robert's first test as he, long since awake, came out of the tent to the drizzle of bacon and beans, and the bubble of coffee in a big black pot.

'Aye,' he said, 'Ye seem to know what you're doin' still,' he added.

That morning, after breakfast, we fished down the river towards Loch Etive just across the mountain from Glencoe. I thought, *What did I do right, to deserve this kind of morning!* Really beautiful country, some of the best in the world. A country of contrast, from the sheer mass presence of the mountain above, to the slender harebells in the heather alongside the crystal-clear river hurrying over red rock as it cascaded towards loch and ocean.

Idyllic and all seemingly peaceful.

I had a copy of a painting by Percy on my wall at home, of Loch Etive more than a hundred years ago, and I wanted to see the exact spot where the mystic beautiful landscape and lochscape had been painted from. It's a restful picture, with distant sheep, charcoal burners and the timeless scene of Highland cattle, the ancestor of the Texas Longhorn. I wasn't disappointed when we eventually did get there, after fishing the river for four hours or so and taking about a dozen nice brown trout just proper enough for lunch, with a bottle of Liebfraumilch which we had left chilling in the water back at the campsite.

The clean fresh highland air was making me hungry. But I was not at all prepared for what happened next to me alone, which I never did mention to Robert.

In some ways, I wish I had now; an 'incompletion'.

We were fishing in a leapfrog pattern about, on the river, two hundred yards apart; too far away to talk but close enough to shout if necessary.

It wasn't.

I had let him catch up at a waterfall about ten feet wide and thirty or forty feet high with a deep pool at the base. Changing intent, I left my rod hidden in the heather, weighted, with the line over the rock edge and into the pool. Not at all proper, I knew that, and why? I wanted to walk around a bit, and was walking slowly from the river to the north and the mountains as he took up his position to sensibly fish the pool.

He looked at my rod with disdain, if not some disgust, and said, 'The trout are not daft, you know!'

What could I do but smile? As I turned towards the mountain, I knew he would take the rod out of the water. The terrain was short grass, some heather and moss, boulder-strewn and sweeping up in a curve quietly and almost geometrically to a scree of small stones and rocks, transitioning to almost vertical and towering rock faces separated by green sweeps up to where the deer are to be found, if you know how.

It was a bright sunny early summer day, sparkling, and now not a breath of wind. There were no insects, just as at sunset, but a few bees floating around the wild flowers carpeting the lower slopes.

I had gone about three hundred years towards the mountain, had turned and was walking, shambling a bit, on the down-slope back to the river. I was in good spirits and relaxed. Suddenly without one second's warning or vague transition of any kind, I was engulfed in panic! The feeling is not unique and has been felt by many people in several parts of the world, but explained by few. Explanations have ranged from a sudden cognisance and compression of personal insignificance to a measurable force spun of physics, excited by the mountain; or a drop or two too much of the local good stuff the night before! I am willing to confess to all three propositions; but there was still another explanation, of a much more 'highland' nature, only a step or two away. My grandmother, who came from Caithness would not have been surprised by these events, but I did, then, wonder what she would have said and thought had she known about the experience. I do know she would have shaken her head and flashed her knowing blue eyes, thinking, *it's all in our head, laddie!*

I had, at that time, survived many tight spots in underground coal in my early days as a British mining surveyor and had long since learned to recognize and suppress any developing panic. We learned to 'cool it' before that became a fashionable phrase. I stopped dead in my tracks and I turned and looked at the mountain. I honestly felt there was something behind me; not a little thing, a big thing. Monstrous. It felt like an emotional avalanche, not roaring down the slope like snow, but an engulfing wash, a not visible field of negative draining energy of source unknown for the time being; something bad, not something good.

Of that I am certain!

I shrugged my shoulders and ate a piece of chocolate and continued to walk down the slope, a bit shaken. I had only gone a dozen yards when I came upon an unusual rock, near the river, blocking my path; structural geology used to be my business, so I stopped to, sort of, look at it. I was still shaking a bit although inside; however my hands were steady as I moved onto the rock surface. The rock was about four feet high or perhaps more; its length as I recall perhaps about fifteen feet. In the center of the rock, which was granite, was curiously an odd-looking shaped hole. It's common for such rocks of harder origins to pick up softer deposits during evolution and then lose the soft material to form a void later. It may have been that, but even now it did not look like that to me. It was too even, too symmetrical, too regular in depth, too many dubious geological coincidences for me in my mood then.

The void in the rock, which was relatively flat in general, was about five or six feet long, about two or three feet in width and twelve inches or more deep. It was filled with six inches of clear rainwater or thereabouts. The rock had been there for a long time now in my opinion; but there was very little moss or even mountain flora on the surface or on the sides or cracks in the rock. It was windswept though. My impression, then, was of a bath, a 'stone bath'. A naturally formed Stone Bath. Just that and most definitely no more! What bothered me a bit was the approximate overall symmetry. Almost straight sides if a mean line was struck through the irregularities and the same as the other side. It really just couldn't be entirely natural. The ends too, were roughly curved by the same irregular deviation from a geometric curve. I had never seen anything like it before, anywhere. In my mind's eye and memory I logged it as an interesting, natural containment for rainwater; handily placed for all those who have passed in the last few hundred years in that glen, to stop and refresh themselves.

Now, twenty years after that visit, I am not so sure of its origins and purpose beyond obvious uses. Enchantment as a function of time and distance was not the case here, but two years ago I saw an almost identically proportioned rough stone shaped the same way, but half scale. It was in Scotland, too, and still is as far as I know.

It was a stone execution block, the only one left in Scotland.

Perhaps not.

ON THE ABILITY TO LET GO WITH STYLE

I tell this story only because my father would have loved it to have been told and shared with others. It concerns some aspects of his own life and, particularly, death and his relationship to me.

He was, in fact, backboned by humor in his day. Early hardened by life and death and later softened by travel, Scottish style.

I think about him often, but I only grieved for him for one day and never again, as he would have wished me to do. He would probably have said that I had wasted one day. I do not see it that way.

I buried him myself, alone, on a beautiful Scottish Friday morning with a firm breeze from the North Sea as company for us both. On that day, I wept for one sweep of the breeze across the cemetery and laughed for an hour later. We both laughed alone that day. For what happened. But then.

We were a lowland Scottish family of good English name. A family of international class sportsmen, really, and this has been an identification more than once. My father, between the wars and as a young man, had found himself a job against the family's wishes. It was almost entirely composed of fun and interest, with little tedium. And he wanted me to know about it. His style.

My father is best imagined as he was, as a young man of the countryside of Scotland. Always well dressed but seemingly most comfortable with a tweed jacket, plus fours and silver cup under his right arm, all balanced by a thorn stick.

He went to war somewhat reluctantly in 1940, in his early thirties – an old man for those days, but the Royal Air Force felt that he could still contribute. So they made him a sergeant in the RAF Regiment and posted him to Regent's Park in London during the Blitz. He told me all about that. There, he drilled and trained young Air Force officers in weapons and unarmed combat, in case they were shot down over the continent.

At the weekends, sometimes he led an officers' dance band from the sergeants' mess. He was an accomplished violinist himself. One evening, he told me later, a young flying officer of Fighter Command came up to him: and said 'Sergeant, my wife's name is Margie, do you think that you could play that for me?' My father replied, 'Certainly, sir, that's a right cheery tune!'

After the war, he returned to his family and his job in Scotland, both including me. I was fourteen at the time and war-weary, too. After a couple of years of adjustment, he decided to take me with him for a week on his job, during my summer holiday from school. I was now sixteen and just capped for wicketkeeping at school, in the footsteps of my uncles, also of the black and gold. He would take me away for a week into his world. I did not know then what a privilege that was and such a given advantage to me for later. We would drive through the country while he conducted his business talking to people. The area we covered, over a few summers, lay between St. Andrews, in Fife, across Perthshire and into Argyle; this was and is incredibly beautiful country which people from all over the world yearn to see and the fortunate pay millions to actually visit.

I saw it all for nothing.

Hell, this was my Dad's territory!

On that first trip, when I was sixteen, we crossed into Perthshire and he started to visibly change. *Relax a bit*, I thought, but also adopt a business air about him. Even his voice, which was normally soft, seemed to spice up a bit. I could see this all clearly as he kept me back among the leather of his faithful long-bonneted Rover. A first class seat you might say. For a first class performance, I might add!

On that day, he did not talk to me all that much. He just seemed to really enjoy the scenery and, perhaps, my company. But what he did say, that day, I sure as hell heard. Soon my father slowed the car down and the long nose of the Rover pushed across the red crunching gravel surface and into the parking area of a nice Scottish country hotel. Red roof, white walls, green ivy and red gravel. Easy on the eye and good for the soul, I thought. He stopped the car, opened up the boot, picked up our two bags and crunched across the gravel with me in tow position behind him. As we reached the granite front step, he turned to me casually and said, *'Imagine anyone getting paid for doing a job like this,'* looking back at me over his glasses.

Well, let me tell you, Sonny Jim!

I had that red ball in my gloves in just one second, and forty feet in the air in another. 'How's that!' I shouted in my mind! He set me up; he really did! Brilliant, I thought, catch them before they get time to set up shop, with your very best ball! I never forgot that tactic in either county cricket for a few years and, of course business later.

Thirty-five years later, on the day he died, I was then a high-flying sales manager, responsible for the country that vastly lies between the Atlantic, Pacific and Arctic Oceans, Canada. *My territory.*

I lived outside Toronto and could have been anywhere, when my Scottish sister called to give me the bad news. The funeral was three days from that day. I made a decision that I should not go. My sister supported that decision. I did not know why, for sure, I made that unusual decision. Fey? I put the phone down, told my wife the news and went straight up to my daughter's now vacant room and locked the door for one day. Then back to work. Ten days later came another phone call from Scotland. This time from a friend of mine from cricketing schooldays. He said, 'Someone has dropped the ball here and your mother needs you'.

I replied, 'Robert, tell her I will be there tomorrow.'

'I'll meet you at the airport,' he said.

He picked me up at the airport on the west coast of Scotland and we drove the seventy miles or so to my mother's home on the east coast. I asked what was wrong, but all he said was, *'She'll tell you by herself.'*

We opened the door of the room and my mother was sitting in a corner chair. She had heard the car coming. She was pleased to see me. She kissed me on the cheek and said, 'I'm glad you're here,' sobbing a bit.

Meanwhile, Robert had poured, quietly, three glasses of sherry, gave one to each of us and left the room. I sat down beside her and said without ado, 'What's wrong, mother?' She looked a bit sad, puzzled and teary. After easily composing herself, she looked me straight in the eyes and said, 'The funeral was a week ago, your father was cremated and your American sister went back to North Carolina a few days ago.' She was trying not to sob and upset me. She continued, 'But the poor man's ashes are in a wee box and nobody knows what to do next.'

She raised her beautiful silver blond head and sipped her favorite Croft sherry. I thought there was just a slight, only slight, twinkle in her eyes. I gave her a pat on the knee and said with steel and deliverance. 'Well, I bloody well do, Mum!'

It was a clear but damp Saturday morning in lowland Scotland, with that peculiar freshness in the air which exiles notice. I decided to scout around the town.

The mortuary was closed.

The cemetery office was closed.

The lawyer's office was closed.

And the undertakers were closed.

But the pubs were not closed, so I visited three of them, gathering information from old friends. After two hours I went back to see my mother. She was sitting just where I left her, waiting for my return expectantly. She looked a bit brighter, I thought at the time. I kneeled down in front of her and looked up at her, patting her knee again and said to her, 'Mother, I will take care of all of this on Monday. It will all be done right, just as you and he would wish.' I added for good measure, 'I know exactly what to do. It's not difficult.'

I am certain that my father, dead as he was supposed to be, started laughing right at that moment! By the following Saturday I had laughed and cried my way across half of Scotland with him, in glorious style!

At nine o'clock on the Monday morning I called for a taxi, asking for someone we had known for some time. When he arrived, twenty minutes later, he said, 'I knew that you would come.' I said, 'Right, Willie, take me out to the mortuary. How's your wife?' He knew exactly what I was here for and did not reply to my enquiry. About ten minutes later, he wheeled the old Humber into the crematorium drive, through a wooded area to the crematorium office. Squeaking to a stop, he just said, 'I'll wait.'

'Right,' I replied.

The office was completely deserted. It seemed a bit strange, so I went through a central corridor and out into a small back yard adjacent to a memorial garden. Right in front of me was a wee small cherubic man looking as if he had jumped out of a jar. He was dressed in a black suit and black shoes and he was covered from head to foot in dust.

For a minute I thought I was transported to the Emerald Isle of old. He skipped forward, smiling and looking as though he had stepped out of a dark flour mill and into the sunshine and greenery of a meadow. He was swiping himself from head to toe alternately with his hands. He looked up purposefully and smiled. 'Mornin', sir,' he said, 'I don't think that I should have scattered the laddie's faither's ashes when there was such a right fair wind off the golf course!' he exclaimed.

I folded my arms and started to laugh as my father would have expected. You see, it was precisely his type of humor. A bulls-eye!

God, I thought, I've come three thousand miles to bury my father and I've burst out laughing on the first day.

With no small effort, I slowed down to a smile and helped him to clean up a bit back in the office. Then he sat down at his desk and quietly we talked for half an hour or so. I explained the situation to him. He understood my needs and told me what to do step by step. I thanked him and left. So then I got into the taxi and visited in town the undertaker, the lawyer and the cemetery. In that order. The undertaker was Scottisheasy and good at his job. Nice and simple soul, a can do man. No fuss, no nonsense. He said, 'Tell us the time, tell us the day, tell us the cemetery, and I'll send a car for you.' He added, 'Don't worry, we will pick up your father's remains for you and we will all go to the cemetery.' At the lawyer's office it was also simple. 'Your father's will is in good order,' he said. 'Your sister in Scotland will look after things concerning disposition, meanwhile if you will give me your signature you can authorize any expenditure related to you father's burial. We have a fund for such situations.' 'Very well,' I said. All nice and simple again, a breeze. So I got back into the taxi and we drove to the cemetery office, Willie still in silence.

'Well, we have six possible grave sites. I will drive you around, personally, now.' So we hopped into his small car and drove around the extensive cemetery where all our people lay in peace. He knew my family.

My response went, 'No, No, No, I don't think so. No.' but then, 'No, wait. Wait a minute here. Please stop the car here.'

On a gently sloping hill, I saw a tree and it was in blossom. It was about twelve feet tall, swaying all the time in the breeze, with blossoms dropping and dancing off to the west as the breeze strengthened noticeably from the sea. I returned to the car and said, 'Mr. Murison, my father will be buried here at nine o'clock on Friday. I will be alone and my mother will not be here for some time.'

Perhaps it was the Golden Flory Cross on the field of blue that I wore with pride, which did it all that day. Or perhaps it was me. All so simple.

I returned to the taxi, returned to my mother's place and said, 'Everything has been arranged, everything is back on track, everything will be done right.'

My father had never spoken all that much to me really. Perhaps he did not think he needed to then.

In any case, soon after my education and training in mining and my marriage to a Fife collier's lassie, I left for Canada. However, I do remember him saying one thing to me on one of our Scottish summer days together.

'Bonnie tree, the hawthorn.'

Before I left him I said, 'Yes, Dad, it gives you everlasting life.'

A STRANGE NOISE IN THE GARDEN

'Gooseberries,' said a soft voice, somewhere close by.

'What is that you said?' I replied, startled, pulling myself up slowly from my garden chair and shading myself with my straw hat from the afternoon sun.

'I said gooseberries. Hummingbirds do not like gooseberries! Apparently it's because they don't have any in Mexico; gooseberries, that is, not hummingbirds, of course.'

I sat up in my garden chair next to the cedarwood honeysuckle trellis and looked around a bit, somehow recognizing the voice from some other time or place, and said simply, 'I am very sorry, I can hear you, but I can't seem to see you,' twisting around left and right in my chair.

'Oh, I'm here all right,' said the voice, 'I'm sitting right behind you on the big flat stone which you set against your garden wall last summer so that you would have a good view across the lake.'

I turned completely around and about ten feet away, behind my wife's perennial garden, there sat, on my stone seat, the big ginger cat who had visited us during the winter.

There he was, sitting with his legs crossed, leaning back against the wall with his big furry paws behind his head and quite relaxed in the summer sun. Somewhat astonished, but not completely surprised this time, I said, 'Genghis Paws, is it not?'

'At your service and the very same cat, sir!' he responded.

'What's all this nonsense about gooseberries then?' I said, a bit sleepily.

'Oh, I was just sitting here with my new friend while you was having your afternoon nap in your garden chair, sir, when I said to him, "Gooseberries." So you understand, sir, this was in response to his enquiry as to what kind of berries those was in your fine kitchen garden,' said the big ginger cat.

'Then,' he continued, 'you see, the hummingbird flew backwards right between his long ears, somewhat alarming him I might say.' He rambled on, 'I was forced to explain that in the hummingbird food chain, they has no link with your gooseberries and that they are Programmed, Primarily for Pink Perennially Pollened Plants, Preferably.'

I said, 'Wait now, Genghis, I do not see or hear any 'new friend' as you talk of.'

'Oh, he's here all right, sir, and besides he hardly ever talks anyway,' said the cat, 'and sometimes never; the reason that you can't see him is that he has moved; he was sitting right beside me here on your stone seat, which is a bit cold, if I may say so, sir. Damp, too. But if you care to look at the grapevine, you will see his two big long brown ears, ahem, wot is listening, while sticking up through the vine leaves. It's too bad that you have to catch him, too; wolfing down your prize grapes; however, he is not quite himself, in his present state. But he did say, sir, that your grapes were considerably better than last year in his opinion. As a matter of fact, Napoleon likes grapes but does not care for your prickly gooseberries,' said Mr. Paws.

'Napoleon, Napoleon?' I said, quite loudly. 'What on earth has Napoleon got to do with this situation?'

'Well sir, now that you have posed the question that particular way, I would have to say, nothing and everything! To do with the situation that is.'

'That is nothing to do with Napoleon the Bonaparte.'

'But everything to do with Napoleon the jackrabbit, wot lives, with his family, in a hole in your golf course wall!'

explained the big cat, now talking on an air which lay somewhere between an investigator, benefactor, legal counsel, and just a plain nosy cat, all puffed up and now standing up beside the stone seat and starting to pace back and forth slowly on the grass walk with his big ginger paws, behind his back, now looking like hot cross buns.

'In my summer capacity,' Mr Paws announced dramatically, then continued, 'as Wildlife Welfare Investigator for Leeds county, I am in the due process of investigating a most unusual case, being that of Napoleon here; who as you can see has taken over one of your garden chairs, upon which I hope you have your name, I might say, and,' he added, 'since Napoleon is more or less a tenant of yours, or vice versa, as the case may develop, I felt the time had come for me to call on you once again to keep you fully informed of this situation – which is quite one of the strangest I have ever investigated in my new capacity.'

After a few moments he continued, while looking up at the blue sky, and waving his head to and fro. 'It seems that Napoleon here has a problem as is often the way of things,' said Genghis Penghis Paws, beginning to tell his story. 'As the squirrel says, without too much imagination, to put it in a nutshell, it seems that he has a problem with both accommodation and food, isn't that so Napper?' he said, looking at the sad jackrabbit for reassurance, the rabbit shrinking in a garden chair with an unusual expression being a combination of guilt, embarrassment, shame.

'Tell me Mr. Paws, just how did you come upon this strange big rabbit?' I said. 'And what is his problem?' I added inquisitively.

'Well, sir, *"ready, always, ready"* is my motto, as you know; learned that in India, I did, and I can assure you that I do not take on assignments indiscriminately, since I am usually campaigning in distant fields of glory,' said Genghis, once again puffing himself up like a giant furry ginger bullfrog.

'Never volunteer unless you must, too busy looking after me,' Paws added, a bit selfishly, I thought. 'Can't look after anybody else if you don't,' he added rather obviously. 'In any case, back to my friend and kindred spirit, you might say, Napoleon,' he said, glancing at the sad-eyed, droopy-eared rabbit.

'It was really strange how we met, sir,' he said. 'As you know I am quite kind, sympathetic and thankfully a very good listener,' he rambled on. 'At least for a big and quite different cat such as I. Had it not been for the latter quality, sorely gained, is the expression, I might not have heard the rather strange noise in the wall, carried by the north wind, it seemed,' he added, ringing a bell in my mind.

'It was coming from the wall by the golf course just beyond the wild garden where the brush wolf lives in the winter time,' said Genghis. 'You see sir, I was minding my own business, as you know is my way when I takes my evening stroll along your golf course wall, savoring the soft evening air redolent with the scent from your honeysuckle tree. A masterpiece of horticulture, I might say,' he continued, somewhat trying my patience with his flattery, albeit well intentioned.

'Well, sir, sweeping my ears and eyes across our fine field, I could not quite pinpoint the source of the sound. My initial thought was that this must be a gang of them field mice with the long tails having one of their noisy gatherings,' said Genghis, now telling his story.

'They do that, you know, hold parties they do, actually get into the wild grape juice laced with strawberry leaves for some reason,' said Paws somewhat explaining the wild situation. 'Rather noisy creatures on occasion, sir, sadly to their demise, I might say; sometimes we sneaks up, surrounds them and eats up the whole party, gourmet style,' he said with some relish. 'Sorry for the apparent digression, sir, but suddenly I spots this oddly triangular hole in your wall behind the tangle of the wild grapevines; sort of a cave, you might say. So I creeps up quietly and fearlessly sticks my head and whiskers into the hole, somewhat surprising them rabbits, I might add.' Genghis stood on his feet showing me the motions.

'Sir, would you believe it, them jackrabbits was sweeping their floor with lily pad leaves, actually eats their brushes afterwards, I understand. Must be into the conservation business as I see it, conservation of themselves first would be my guess,' added Genghis, swanning around with his story. 'Good evening, animals,' I says, not knowing what they was for sure, since it was a bit dark. This really startled the lot. 'Genghis Paws is my name, the famous cat from Leeds county,' I added, to introduce myself properly and in a gentlemanly fashion. 'My, what a really fine house you have here, with all them stones and stuff,' I says for good measure, a butter-up, since I was outnumbered. 'But pray tell me just what is all this noise about on this fine spring evening,' I says waiting for an answer.

'Well, sir, if you can believe it, the big jackrabbit you see before your very eyes pipes up with his problem,' continued Paws. 'His house got flooded, it seems, in the late winter and spoiled all his spring food supply. A sad situation sir, a very sad situation, considering all them other rabbits that were hiding in his back room. Being highly observant, I could just see them, sir, although it was a bit dark in their house as I said; six pairs of seemingly yellow eyes peeking out of their back room. Evaluating the facts quickly, this of course immediately alerted me to the seriousness of the situation, sir, which I had stumbled upon during my evening stroll along your wall. Waterlogged house and at one time semi-submerged rabbits is not a happy thought to cats such as I,' said Paws benevolently.

I interrupted the big, but intelligently babbling cat quickly and said, 'Genghis, this is all very interesting, really, but what led to this quite unfortunate state of affairs?'

'Well, sir, as I see it, there are two primary factors in this interesting case and eight different rabbits, or even more at Easter, I understand. The reason that Napper is so quiet this morning is that it seems that their entire winter food supply was nefariously nicked from your good lady wife's cultivated prize ve-g-e-t-a-b-l-e garden,' said Genghis, finally identifying the problem precisely. 'A bit much, I would say, if asked; nicking other people's vegetables and staying in other people's walls. You know, there is nothing more distressing or in such poor taste in life that an opportunistic rabbit with a transparent plan to the clear detriment of other species, I always says.'

The big cat rambled on as I tried to listen.

'However it's not for me to say too much, in this case or others, as I have been known to take possession myself of other people's stuff, without a formal invitation to do so, you might say,' Genghis confessed for some mysterious reason.

'Just simply a question of survival at the time, when it really comes down to it,' he said, continuing to spin his yarn. 'Nothing much more than that. According to my overnight investigation, it seems they were all in this garden plot together,' reported the big cat capsulizing his basis for proceeding further.

'As I visualize it, a strange sight it must have been on that moonlit early September night with all them rabbits looking like a caravan crossing the desert; hauling away your lettuce, radishes, leeks, cauliflower, cabbage, beetroot, peas, beans, onions and more than just a few of them really long English c-u-c-u-m-b-e-r-s! Even stole your wheelbarrow for a while, I understand, four rabbits on each handle must have been the way, I deduce. I am just surprised that them criminals, we have to call them, sir, did not quietly break into your fine home and nick the house dressing when they was at it; most surprising I must say, and shows a lack of ingenuity and class,' said Paws, not letting me get a word in edgewise, in case I spoiled his story, no doubt.

'Genghis, this is just a quite amazing story and piece of investigation, and I am not sure what I should say, or what punishment should be meted out,' I said to the cat, establishing my position quite clearly.

'Well, sir, that's a noble, but strictly a human thought; you must realize, however, fate, fortune and, as usual, mainly mysterious cataclysmic circumstances have already punished them rabbits quite enough,' said Genghis, with some grain of wisdom, I thought. 'You see, sir, one of them rabbits is definitely, I have to conclude, somewhat reluctantly, just a bit bent, we might say; the big little one with blue eyes which just happens to be looking out of their house door over yonder,' said Paws pointing a great big furry paw now as big as a muffin, towards the wall covered with vines.

'He is a really big strong lad, too, by all accounts, which complicates things a bit in dealing with him, but definitely the rabbit which made the serious error leading to the flooding of their food supply. I have several witnesses to this particular aspect of the crime. Of course, you must understand, sir, none of us like blowing the whistle on our other animal friends unless we have to,' said Paws, rounding out his point of view.

'Seems that after these, thieves, we have to call them now ,sir, stole your prize vegetables, that great big lump of a rabbit went back to the scene of the crime and hijackrabbited a thirty foot length of your green garden hose. This accidentally branched them into a new dimension of mischief; you see the hose was froze full of ice since your good lady wife forgot to turn off the tap on your house wall in the late fall, as is her way upon occasion, as you well know and I have observed.'

Listening to all of this tale was beginning to make me wonder about things. Perhaps about time, too.

'Of course, a froze hose in the spring sun, is all it took to render their salad somewhat soggy, and sadly so,' continued Genghis. 'It's all rather silly sir, when you think of it. If you think of it.' said the big cat, his voice now drifting away.

'Pointless, perhaps. Rabbits and everything, I mean. Reflections of the summer sun, I dare say, all of us. After all, who really wants gooseberries anyway? Gooseberries, gooseberries, gooseberries!'

'Where is my basket of gooseberries?' said a voice somewhere close by.

SO YOU WANT TO BE A LEADER?

A good friend of mine lives in Northumberland county in Ontario, Canada.

He lives in a house on a hill and everyday he goes walking.

A year or two ago, I went walking with him and I told him that I intended to write a short story for a collection, based on one of his experiences and also relate it to business just a bit, and leadership.

I said, 'I want to tell them about the finest hour of the *Me, Too!*'

He said, 'That's okay. Just so long as all the nice things you say are, in fact, me and anything else is not me. Also the *Me, Too* was my wife's idea.'

I said, 'Ronald, you're on!'

A general officer or a general manager maybe, or any of the other thousand ways to be one. A leader that is. Or maybe even reversing the situation and wondering, in retrospect, why you were not? Or didn't want to be.

Not many are, will be or were.

Some people, seemingly well qualified, are too smart, too late or perhaps even afraid to be leaders. Leadership's price tag is responsibility, at any level. If things go well, the laurels are yours, but if things go wrong, you are to blame and no one else. A leader knows that. Good leaders are quite rare and I think that most of them are born that way and training is the track they follow to opportunities.

Leaders are a bit like cherries in a fruit salad; they are easily seen but hard to find. Usually leaders are identifiable at an early age, often in school systems, through various accomplishments and peer recognition.

They do tend to stick out and usually have this and that to prove it. To be a leader at sixteen and to be a leader still at forty or even sixty is the result of a combination of versatility, opportunity, desire, tenaciousness, timing and being in the right place, at the right time, with the right bag of tricks. Milady Luck, in other words; the undefinable, unexplainable group of circumstances that brought person to place; serendipity will do for now.

Many of the best leaders are never found, or at least lost to recognition, and close doesn't count, with leaders and their expectations of themselves and others.

Foxy, second best leaders have been known to take them out of play, in many organizations, but so what of that? A leader has to produce results and win, with real gamesmanship being the common denominator in all leaders, be they political, commercial, military or financial, or anything else, too, and it is an art learned by practice only. A leader not only has to be qualified beyond question, but if they don't know how to play the game, they will eventually lose to someone who does.

While on our walk on the hill in Northumberland County, my friend asked me what the *Me, Too* had to do with leadership, and I responded that he already knew really, but had not recognized that factor which is rarely discussed in books or business management. I also added that I had discussed this factor with several company presidents in the United States and Canada and all of them said that they had forgotten to properly address this facet of leadership on the way up the ladder.

He said, 'Well, what was it?'

I told him then and now I will tell you!

If you can't sail, don't have a boat and don't have the time, how do you become the commodore of an exclusive yacht squadron in five years?

Well, let me tell you that my friend couldn't, didn't, didn't and did!

He did have some things going for him, however. He lived close to a city which had a well established yacht club on one of the Great Lakes. Inland seas is a better term. He did have various business connections and contacts around the city. This is an asset to progress anywhere. He was sociable, polished and presentable, also eager to learn. He also could afford to buy a good boat; that helps, too! Just why he wanted to join the yacht club I am not quite sure and he never told me. So I will have to make it up, sort of, and also how he did it.

Well, he observed, as many do, that some people have a better time than others, largely because they made this happen to their own advantage but also to the benefit of others, too. Since he did tell me once that, in business, making friends and then using them was fair play. This, of course, is a fact of life. You've got to know people, the right people, to get ahead. Simple, time-honored methodology. Just as location, location, location is the banner of merchandising and property. Connections, connections, and connections is the long pennant at the mast of marketing, a boat which we both sailed.

As of a summer afternoon he also noticed that while others were slaving away at this and that, some people were swanning around the azure, under colorful spinnakers with a vodka and tonic close at hand. This made a lot of sense to my friend. I know that, and why not, after all?

I am still not sure whether the gallery of portraits of resplendent past commodores of the club had anything to do with his 'end game plan' but I think that it did. Visualization is a critical facet to progress; we were both US trained and he understood that clearly. He saw himself up there first, I would wager and win.

He was right in his approach, I can tell you, too, and he looks splendid in his portrait, just like a billy-be-damned blue water salt with blue blazer and crested gold cap.

I should say also that he was never a half measures man and he knew that the only way to get anything done right was to do every step correctly in the right order for eventual success.

He reads quite a bit, too, so he did all his homework on any aspect of sailing and socializing. He and his wife's enthusiasm and organizational skills could be applied, too, to all aspects of the yacht club's activities, from fund-raising, through Christmas parties, to barbecues and races around the Bay. In short they were assets to the club. He trained, with his wife in a friend's boat, so that they both understood the rudiments of sailing, and it was not too long before he bought an eight meter boat.

It was audaciously christened the *Me, Too* in the usual style. The name was his wife's idea and is a tribute to her sense of humor and understanding of her husband and my good friend.

Over a year or two, just everybody knew the *Me, Too* and her crew. Nice boat. Nice people and proven assets to the operations of the Yacht Club.

He participated in the races round the bay and studied the way of wind and waves. He noted the tricks of the trade and the successful and unsuccessful action of the other boats over time.

Soon, too, he could socialize and sail quite respectably and was given increasing responsibility, and he also assumed authority where necessary. That's how it's done, after all. My friend liked this whole waterborne culture. Al least for a while.

He really did enjoy the racing and managed to hold his own, as he had a really good boat and growing confidence. He even took the *Me, Too* on a five hundred mile sail around the lake during the summer, calling on both Canadian and US yacht squadrons. Great stuff with new friends, easily made for an affable couple.

He also enjoyed spending the night on his boat under the stars, with the anchored boat tied to one of the buoys, as he enjoyed margaritas and music. Nor did he complain when he fell into the bay in his pajamas. Soft he is not and he has medals to prove it, and he still goes back to France to smell the lavender and remember a boy with a parachute in the night sky.

As time went by, he continued to get better at racing, but he never really took it seriously. He is good. He enjoyed competing in the wind and waves and, being mechanically minded, took easily to roping the ropes, shifting the canvas and tacking round the bay.

I asked him a few years ago if he ever placed in a race, as this would be quite an achievement with thirty boats and experienced competitors, some deep sea experienced. His answer was, 'Yes, sure I did,' being modest as usual for him. 'I placed fourth a few times and sometimes third. Hell, I was first once!'

'Were you really? How did you manage that?' I asked.

He said, 'Well, I was in second place towards the end of the race and I did the right thing with a wind gust and passed an astonished commodore on the inside, just missing the marker buoy.'

I said, 'Well, what then?'

He responded, 'I held the lead for about two or three minutes, slackened off sail just a bit and let him pass!'

I said, 'C'mon, now, that's not you. You were bloody well trained to give no quarter in such a situation, especially to a commodore!'

'You're right, you're right,' he said.

'Well, what then?' I pressured.

'To tell you the truth, I didn't know where to go. You see I had just always followed the other boats and buoys out in front of me while racing. I really hadn't thought about what to do or where to go if I was in the number one position!'

Sometime later I told him that the company presidents I had talked to had all been in the same boat! They all said that when they got there they were all surprised at what the task actually involved. I said to him, 'Maybe it's a good thing to know where you're going before you hoist your sails.'

He replied, 'Yes, that's true enough, but it doesn't quite seem to work that way. Things change, and unknown factors at the start come into play by the finish.'

'Maybe, then,' I said, 'it's essential that you do not know what to do before you get there,' and I added, 'to be a good leader. No preconceived ideas, I mean.'

'That could be right,' he said, 'that could be right. Wanna buy a boat and go for a sail?'

'Sounds good to me, skipper,' I said.

'Atlantic or Pacific, or the North-West Passage?'

THE VESSEL

Oriented to the winds with low elevation.

Smooth crafted, long and narrow, please, flexible, too, would be good.

Transverse ventilation is a must. Quite cool.

Expect the sun to rise on the starboard quarter.

Major axis to the east north east, s'*il vous plait*.

I would think some reach in the prow and modest to the stern.

Can't be too careful here and now, experience to the fore.

Accommodations for a maximum in summer and minimum in winter not necessarily so here.

However, must be provisioned well at all times, gentlemen.

Clearwater drawn deep and all systems below decks.

Climate and weather sharp.

Forty meters long for headway and eight meters beam for stability.

Celsius forty, both ways.

That should do it!

This distillation may be close to that given to the long-housed Huron some time ago, and also perhaps to the *arpenteur* who laid down our vessel, too.

Which beats well in all weather, I have found.

Sometimes lost in the shimmer of the summer heat waves, or becoming a long motionless iceberg in winter.

Seen, at a cable's length, just like a frigate; behind ravelins of snow and captured by the ice.

Sometimes, too, with Merryweather lights twinkling and hoots from the January men.

Through the glass, on the prow, the polestar high.

A cold friend, on watch and waiting as we do.

Like us a vessel, on a voyage, in a fleet of Winken Blinken ships,

Never to catch up with anything.

Too silent, witness to grief from the ground and sorrow from the sea.

The first mate, me and the ship's cats, all lost in such order and beauty.

Pass on the port, ma'am; if you please.

OWEN SOUND OWEN

Now I'll bet that you folks probably never heard tell o' Garnet Owen.

It's kind of a long story, so to squeak, which I will have to shorten up, about a world famous pig farmer hereabouts.

Now this feller was real unusual and ripsnorted his way through life better than most, since somewhere along the line he got the curiously convenient idea in his head that there were only seven commandments. Smart fella!

I first knew him when he bought a spread about fifteen miles due north of Owen Sound (I guess we should have known). Anyway he sure as hell got our attention and showed that he was different from the likes of us after the day he showed up at the market with two sows sittin' in the backseat of an old Rolls Royce motor car. Gar had the gentleman's glass partition drawn 'sows' they couldn't breath down his neck; practical feller with a touch of class, I always thought.

Well, sir, whatever Gar wasn't, he was the damndest pig farmer I ever did meet: his claim to fame was that he eventually bred the longest pig in the world – twenty-three feet seven from front to back – called her Isabella, as I recall, after his mother-in-law; Yes, sir, so he did…

Now Gar, as you can see, had a different idea from most of us on how to set about things, but where he first got the idea about breedin' them long pigs is still something of a mystery in Snyder township, except to me.

Lookin' back, I suppose it must have all started when Gar and his kin started keepin' to themselves, you might say. Don't suppose it was till the two boys came into town and bought a forty foot length of iron culvert and three skateboards that the folks here began to think Gar was up to somethin' more than just unusual.

Isabella was the damndest sow I ever did see, longer than the welcome wagon, and she turned the corner of the barn by stoppin' her front legs and marchin' in a sweep with 'er back legs 'till everythin' was lined up again in a new direction.

(I guess we should have known...)

Too bad that Gar only showed her once; as I recall they both started 'bout the same time: late that winter.

Soon after Isabella was gone Gar took ill, too, and the talk in town was that he was takin' on real bad, so I went up to his place, seein' that it didn't look as though he'd be around that much longer.

Well, sir, I sat at that feller's bedside and asked him straight how he ever got started breedin' them long pigs.

It slowly came out that one day he was feedin' the pigs when he noticed that one sow was just a tad longer than she should have been. He said that he never thought about it too much at the time, but a few weeks later he surefire saw that this gal was definitely gittin' longer instead o' fatter, as intended by mother nature. According to Gar she grew to be nine feet one and a bit long, all by herself, you might say; Gar knew right there and then that breedin' long pigs instead o' fat ones might be the way to set himself apart from the likes of us.

Seems that even Gar never dreamed even then that a few years later he would breed the longest long pig in the whole damn world: Isabella; like I said, 'bout twenty-three feet seven inches in a hot sun or even twenty-three in a cold culvert, so she was.

Well, sir, sittin' there at his bedside (it was rainin' on the panes, as I recall), I thought that there must be a helluva lot more to it than he was tellin', so I whispered to him as he lay there, eyes closed and in real bad shape, 'Gar,' I said, 'You just gotta let me tell the folks how you really bred them long pigs, t'ain't right nor fittin' that you don't now.'

Well, sir, sure as the sun rises and sets on the US of A and other good places he opened one eye and whispered, 'Nuthin' to it, really – every mornin' the hired hands grabbed 'er by the ears and the two boys grabbed a hind leg apiece, they dug in their heels in that red, rusty Georgia-style dirt and just pulled 'er like to beat hell. Stretched her 'bout an inch every day, so they did.'

Well, sir, Garnet Owen passed over and out right there and then with a smile on his face. So if you're still there, Mabel, readin' all this foolishness and you don't smile a bit – just like Owen Sound Owen did – the very next time you see any sow, or especially a sow just a tad longer than she should be, then I ain't writin' no more stories for yer.

'Fifteen miles north of Owen Sound; where in the hell is that, Albert? Feller might 'av bin pullin' them pigs and my leg. Do feel a little taller come to think of it!'

'Isabella...? Nice ring to it.'

AMERICANS AND THE GEORGIA BUS

'Would y'all like a donut, son?' said the American operating a
bakeshop-like stainless steel gadget dropping perfectly formed
dough into a deep pan of boiling oil.

'Well, thank you, mister. We call them doughrings here and
I haven't seen one for five years.'

'Well, then, you're all set now, son.' said the sailor on board
the USS Helena, a cruiser visiting the east coast of Scotland
over fifty years ago.

A most welcome sight then.

This was the very first American I ever met. My first
impression of Americans was favorable, an impression I was
never to change after working with them and for them, too, for
thirty years. Not as a Scot but as a Canadian, traveling and
plain just doin' business across North America. Boston, New
York, Chicago, Clearwater, New Orleans, Savannah or San
Antonio. America, I found, is just brimming full of surprises
and exciting all the time, in every state, both night and day.

The back roads of New York State, South Carolina. New
Hampshire or Colorado have to be explored, too, along with
the West Virginia 'hollers', the Florida flare or the places along
the Ohio or Mississippi river valleys.

There, Americans are so often quite different from the
residual view left of these people in foreign countries;
sometimes by manipulated images shaped, seeded and filtered
to suit commercial or political purpose. It's too bad.

116

After all, how many Americans do you know? I mean personally, in their country; in their kitchens, in their offices, at their ball games or in their schools or prayer meetings. Don't be ashamed to disqualify yourself or have to think again. It works both ways – between all countries.

In America, surprises happen with a boom, I think. It may not be so for some; but that's the way it was for me. A sudden grasp of a simple reality related to more complex circumstances later.

They say something, you listen and understand and you're in!

Boom!

You say something, you haven't listened and you're out. Bang! Boom, you're in, bang you're out, nice and simple. The American way, in a different form, and in my view it's a good idea to listen while you're in America for a prolonged length of time.

Believe me, you have got to get it!

'When you folks come to Harrisburg, Pennsylvania, mister, we'll give you a paragraph in our local newspaper – but if you leave town, we'll give you a whole page!'

Boom!

'Mistah, there ain't nothin' old in Denver, Colorado!'

Boom!

'Goin' to Philadelphia, son, don't you forget to have a cheesesteak – welcome to America and also don't forget to enjoy yourself, too!' said the customs man at the airport.

Boom!

'Ah, sure am sorry, sir, but ain't nobody ever really counted all them coal mines in these West Virginia woods – tho' I hear tell it's close to three thousand big and small!'

Boom!

'Welcome to Alabama, mistah,' said the old gal in dusk, drivin' the cab. 'You Canadian, eh? Mighty fine ball park y'all

117

got up there in Toronto! You be sho' to have some of our famous BA-BEE-Q ribs while you heah.'

Boom!

'Sorry, mistah, but this is Dallas and ain't nobody comes to have a good time here in a shirt and tie.' – snip – snip – 'Now you pin that tie on that big wall over yondah so that all the folks kin see you're goin' to have a good time and remembah your visit to a Texas steakhouse!'

Boom!

All operatin' instructions on how to do business and get along in 'we're right here' America. Like I say, boom! and suddenly you are there! It's them – the real Americans, revealing themselves to you. You're in, you begin to understand.

Still, a new nation, with depth, compassion, vitality and wealth, and as they might say in the Deep South and much 'Bowcoo savvy they ain't even used yet!'

Now, 93°F in Atlanta, Georgia Airport, with back soaking humidity, salted up through Mobile from the Gulf of Mexico, the Delta shuttle, the Georgia bus.

I am enroute to Alabama, they are going to another gulf a world away. Four of them, soldiers, still in Brookes Brothers and L.L. Bean wool and cotton.

Relaxed outside, tense inside; career men, family men, school men, peaceful men and silent. Reserve officers in the United States Army.

Reporting!

All big men, with already short-cropped hair, leaving their jobs and families to keep their promises to their country.

Later, in the same Southern day, hotter still in Columbus, Georgia, near Fort Benning. Now a hotel lobby and coffee shop near the airport.

A swarm of uniformed infantry soldiers, men and women. At every table, at every desk, on every carpeted step, cramming out of elevators and spilling out of doorways into the asphalt parking areas outside. All enlisted young Americans. God, eighteen-year-olds again. Shined up and polished boots in contrast to their soft, sandy desert outfits.

'You're lucky to get a room here, mistah!' said the clerk at the reception desk. 'Six thousand soldiers have passed through this place in one month, can you beat that? This lot are movin' out, more comin' in the afternoon. Noisy, ain't they, mistah?'

Some were noisy, some were not, I observed, as I waited for my room to be cleaned up by the maids.

'Have a donut and coffee while you're waiting,' said the reception desk clerk, pointing to a long table covered by a white cloth and laden down with coffee urns, pitchers of orange and grapefruit juice, donuts and sweet rolls, plus cartons of milk and dozens of packets of breakfast cereal.

Boom! again.

One young man, alone, at a table, near the door, his eyes easily read. I decided to do so first: then I walked across, smiled at him, put my hand on his shoulder and said only, 'Don't worry, you'll be all right, soldier. Have a donut!'

'Thank you, mister,' he said, standing up tall.

Boom!*

---

* Out of consideration for my American friends and their tragedies and my writing style i.e. the use of the word *boom*. This story was written on September 15 1998.

THE CHRISTMAS BIRDS

Where we live in the Northern Lakes and woods, we have visitors all year round; from the south in the spring and from the north in the autumn.

The same beautiful birds each year.

These visitors join our resident birds, our winter companions, at various times throughout the year. They arrive always in the same order and nearly always in the same week and always welcome.

Even our seven cats like them, too.

These birds range from the Canadian Arctic to the Gulf of Mexico and include brilliant orange orioles, red cardinals, blue jays, purple and yellow finches, also flashing green hummingbirds and steel blue swallows.

Yellow eastern meadowlarks strut across our lawn and Maurin doves coo around the eaves of the house. Even tree dwelling wood ducks squawk from the marshland, while red-tailed hawks dash past our windows, trying to steal mice from our cats in an endless summer game. Blue herons float by with disdain, as do the occasional bald eagles and ospreys. Giant white gulls who have never seen the sea crowd the golf course greens like a daybreak muster. In our long hedgerows, under the profusion of wild grapes and raspberry growth, both partridge and pheasant roam safely protected from predators.

Each spring from Mexico, mosquito-catching barn swallows stage a flypast past our windows, being a signal for me to open the boathouse door under my bedroom, so they, as generations before them, can nest for the new families amid the clutter of the old oak beams.

All these birds and many more enrich our lives daily and provide nature's way of reminding us of passing time. They come, they go, on the highroad of the winds. Tiny birds you can hardly see and mighty birds, whose shadows can cross the garden, stirring a feeling of primitive alarm for just a second or two.

In this part of Canada, the arrowheads of geese go south in October, usually trailing all other birds on the first of the cold winds. By November, all of our summer visitors are gone, leaving only our resident birds; the blue jays, chickadees, woodpeckers, some hawks and sparrows, too.

Strangely and most curiously, the most exotic bird has yet to come to visit on the way south. I call them the 'Christmas birds' because they do not arrive until December, when the snow lies heavy on the ground and on the conifers. They are the gentlest of all our birds, with tailored sleek plumage, in appearance like a gray morning suit and red carnation. They are cultured, civilized and with almost immaculate manners. They pay their respects, a flock of one hundred, by covering two mountain ash trees, still laden with orange berries. They twitter in a singsong manner, almost magically passing berries to each other sometimes, with ceremony and poise.

The mountain ash is known as the rowan in Scotland, and in highland Scotland the rowan is historically a most mystic tree. So here in Canada we have magic birds and a mystic tree.

When the cold winds take the birds of prey south and snow covers nature's predators, the beautiful cedar waxwings come to visit in safety. Quiet birds, happy birds, peaceful birds, and once friends to the king of Spain.

Our birds for Christmas.

THE GOLF COURSE DUCK

Everyone knows, now, that when a tree falls naturally in the woods and there is nothing there to, let's say, hear it, or pick up the vibrations, there is no sound. Simple, gosh, physics! Even the speed of light has long since been energetically squared and factored with mass. Perhaps not quite so simple physics.

However, far more complex are ducks on the golf course. I live next to both and I know it's not so simple as mere science. I know, for just about every day, as right now, I can hear the golf course duck quacking. It's exactly like a person laughing, as I listen. It's a laugh, I tell you!

The duck is, in fact, laughing and no wonder; at golfers especially, but the duck laughs, no doubt, at all of us most times.

I should say that although I have lived next to the golf course for about ten years, I have never actually seen the aforementioned golf course duck, but it is there. Pairs of ducks do fly by my window quite often, but I do not think any of them are the golf course duck. Here, black and lonely loons wail in the night and Great Lakes gulls, lost forever, cry in the early morning mists, but the golf course duck only laughs in the afternoon sun. I like that. It's no wonder, too, and sometimes he laughs long into the afternoon in September at friends of mine

'How was your game today?' I asked a visitor to our place a few years ago. 'Not bad,' he said, 'not bad at all. Well, except for the hole down by the big pond.' Oh, God, not again, I thought, with visions of ducks scattering across the green or laughing from the moss and flower-carpeted woods; surely not again?

You see, a year before that, on a September afternoon, too, at the pond hole green, something, dare we say, unusual happened. It seemed quite innocent at first, as another friend and visitor played a lofted shot over the trees, laser straight, high and with perfect range for the pond hole green, just slightly to the right of the hole itself. About one hundred and sixty yards to walk on a nice day. But when he reached the green, only his partner's ball was visible about five feet from the hole; an excellent shot and first class golf.

After a search he found his ball in the hole. A bit embarrassing in golf, the game of, as they say, well, a lob, two bounces, a kick off a twig and a roll to the hole; it happens, but not often, most never, or hardly ever at least. But it is explainable, on most golf courses. Not so easily explainable on a golf course with a duck who laughs in the woods in the afternoon sun.

Later, the remarkable shot was discussed in the clubhouse.

An elderly retired military man, one of many around here, announced with authority, 'It was undoubtedly the duck! The duck picked up the ball and placed it in the hole, don't you know?'

'I've seen it meself!' he said. 'Sounds incredible, but it's probably the same duck! Must be!' he reasoned, upsweeping his trim moustache. Well, now that had seemed final enough!

Was the score four on three then, or what was the question posed? Three it remained, but was it correct or even right? There was doubt. The question was posed again later that day to me at my house. I confessed that I really did not know the answer, but the ball was in the hole, so the score should be three, notwithstanding the accused duck.

However, I did say that I would get a ruling on this from my sister in Scotland, who lives near St. Andrews. In fact, I would call her right away. She plays golf quite a bit, was captain of her club then, and quite authoritative about the game in general. So

I phoned. She was there and never surprised at the actions or questions of her brother at strange hours, she listened to the problem on the golf course.

'I'll have to get my wee book,' she said sleepily, after listening to my story. She returned to the phone and said, 'According to my interpretation of the Rules of the Royal and Ancient Golf Club at St. Andrews, the score is definitely three!' She added, 'If the duck did, in fact, put the ball in the hole, the score is still three! You have to understand that if no one actually *saw* the duck put the ball in the hole, then it didn't, even if it did.' She closed. After a pause she asked, 'Is that quite clear to you?' dusting me with a dose of her superior intellect.

I answered, 'Yes, er, ma'am, sis, it is clear to me. What it means is that as long as you don't see what's going on it's really all right. Even if it's wrong.'

'That does seem to be the way of things,' said my sister, recovering her Scottish sense of humour and couth. 'But it is bad manners to laugh, even for a duck!'

I did not tell my friend the story from the previous year, but he did expand that day on his experience at the pond hole. I had hoped that he wouldn't!

'Yes,' he said, 'I played a beautiful shot, pin high! It should have been about ten feet from the hole and on the green. Funny thing; found the damn ball, forty feet from the hole and in the pond!'

'Yes, it is a funny thing,' I said. 'By the way,' I ventured, 'did you hear anything unusual when you picked up the ball?' I looked carelessly at the ceiling.

'No,' he said, 'Can't say I did. No, now, wait a minute, there was something!'

'I thought so,' I mumbled, tapping into his thoughts.

'By the way, sir,' he added, 'do you keep ducks, by any chance?'

SUNDOWN SAUCE

It doesn't matter how I start, how I finish or what I put in; all my sauces and soups turn out to be red and spicy! Almost all, that is.

I really don't know why. Maybe it's just the predominance and availability of locally grown produce, including field tomatoes and various red peppers, plus a personal *penchant* for the wines of France and Italy. Red, of course.

I, like many other kitchen dabblers, don't use recipes in the conventional way; well, perhaps a glance now and again for general 'do's and don'ts', but that's about it and it's more than enough at that. What's there and handy is what goes into my soups and sauces; the more ingredients, the more fun is my discovery.

Once, and only once, did my sauce not turn out red and I really don't know why, either!

Sauce making or soup making, for me, is a relaxation. A diversion for a beautiful autumn morning especially. As a means of deflecting the mind, it is superior to many forms of meditation, in my opinion. It relaxes the mind, body and soul without, well, just sitting there on a cushion looking suspiciously like having an advanced nap.

I tend to favor reasonably priced Beaujolais as an important element and ingredient of this entire process. In fact, it is essential!

The only thing that needs to be known about Beaujolais is that the *nouveau* is more interesting, somehow, for this purpose, and also the fact that it never goes into the soup or sauce.

It's autumn wine for autumn people! With autumn thoughts!

With all my sauces and soups, I do not decide which until a certain point in the whole procedure. It adds interest!

Begin with a heated, wide and deep pan. This is so you have a clear panoramic view of the developing creation and do not have to peer into a deep pot. Common kitchen sense. Well, it's also more surface and more even heat, too!

Best butter or good olive oil goes into the pan first, and garlic! Then chopped onions or shallots, also chopped red and green peppers are added to the sizzle. Now in my scheme of things, when the kitchen fills with the aroma of the basic vegetables of the brew, I add either fresh or tinned tomatoes. Italian style are best. Now to the red *potage*; I add about ten dabs of Louisiana hot sauce, the best quality available and also red. In fact again, everything is red so far.

Now the decision has to be made. Is this to be a soup or sauce? The decision is critical, so a goblet of Beaujolais is sipped while looking out the window at the maple trees changing to red. Mmm! I wonder if it's the trees?

The decision was sauce! Can't say I know why, but I do know! I now know it's going to be a sauce! Sauce *formidable!* No shilly-shallying. Not the shadow-like sauces of some parts of Europe, but something to demolish strong game; where they just knock off the horns and wheel her to the table!

Saddle sauce... campaign Sauce... man Sauce...!

Sundown sauce!

Condiments such as curry powder and Texas chili powder are good combinations of several spices and are very convenient to use in the Saturday morning kitchen. I always use both! Had I decided to make soup I would have added chicken, preferably, or beef stock at this point, since sauce it is to be; I use seasonal fruit. In my case, this means peaches or apricots and apples, but definitely not citrus fruit such as oranges or lemons. I don't know why about that, either!

After adding the chopped fruit to the sauce-to-be, I add two teaspoonfuls of Firehouse chili powder or equivalent and one teaspoonful of Sharwood's hot curry powder. To balance the acidic tomatoes, I add a good measure of either brown sugar or maple syrup. Not white sugar or corn syrup if you can avoid it. I do know about that!

After pouring another goblet of Beaujolais, I stir the brew slowly till it is all thoroughly mixed and lightly cooked on a low fire, and then I always check my wife's kitchen cupboard for interesting ingredients just to separate sundown sauce from all of the other sauces.

I see a bottle of mushroom ketchup. Ah, forest food! Wo ho! Definitely a fit with the plan, a good dollop of this!

What's this. Wild grape jelly, why not? Dark and mysterious, perhaps a tablespoonful or two would be about right. No doubt about it, it's a sauce to run with the bulls!

Another sip of Beaujolais and stirring gently; sniff, sniff, the kitchen now filling with a vaguely familiar pungence. Woops! Now, it's suddenly settled and smoothed. The moment of truth; not one other ingredient must be added, just a little stirring and slow cooking for consistency.

Well, now this *is* different, it's getting darker; in fact, a smooth, speckled dark brown. Tasting time, I think, soon. While I always stir my sauces with a wooden spoon, I always taste them with a silver spoon. Why? Well, it's ceremonious.

The sauce looks right, nice and smooth, smells interesting, too. It's strong plus, no doubt about that, too bad it's brown, though, instead of red. Well, no matter, let's taste it anyway!

Mm... mm, not bad, not bad at all. Does seem familiar, though. It's strong, brown, too, same consistency. What's it called? *Sauce Robert?* No, it can't be, it's not possible, one chance in a thousand. I am no *saucier*. But it is! Astounding; unmistakable, classic pepper pungent. The Thames River sauce of England. Stored in the Houses of Parliament, no less! Everybody knows its name.

Sundown sauce, of course!

MEG'S REVENGE

No cannon from Liege;
    Forged in bronze and passion flayed iron,
    Ensconced within Edinburgh's walls to answer then, at the
gate,
    Norham's insolence.
    Nor a seaborne Queen to bond a Kingdom fair.
    Not Meg.
    She did not know that to be poor and different was a sin.
    Nor fear the only weapon of greed and power.
    Not Meg.
    She shunned the day and sang in the night.
    She came in the hodden dusk and left in the blaze of dawn.
    She did not forget,
    She did not forgive,
    She did not die.
                       Nor Will?
               ...and...Not Meg?

THE COMPANY MEN

It was quite dark inside and with a smoky atmosphere. Dimly lighted by two oil lamps with scalloped brass reflectors. Light, too, from an open fireplace with shadows dancing all around the whitewashed stone walls.

No spark of coal here, nor crackling Xmas logs, but only the smouldering fire of a patient man.

The cottage was small with a low roof of thatched straw. The roof was weighted in places by hemp ropes and wire of drawn steel, with large stones attached. The straw was almost black from peat smoke. The feeling within the single room with an alcove was one of warmth and simplicity. It was a one person house, not a home, at least it was now. I had nothing better to do as I sat by the fire but look around and listen. So, that's what I did. Beside the fireside chair was a low circular oak table and about twelve feet away was a much larger table with three chairs, and to the side of the table was the alcove. It was screened by a heavy patterned curtain on outsized brass loops attached to a plain wooden rail. The curtain was almost drawn, but reddish brown army blankets showed underneath a heavy goosedown quilt of some quality: in the corner of the quilt, initials – JP. On the large table was a large green blotting pad, some pens, and a bottle of blue ink. There were about a dozen sheets of good writing paper. There were also two black leather books, new, which looked like desk diaries. They were both elegant, with a silver shield or crest; one had a silver clasp, closed, and the simple initials GBR. Also on the table, a tiny flask, maroon, leather-bound and silver, too – they meant nothing to me. Then. There was also a large cedar chest, far from home I would think; it was exceedingly plain with no markings at all. Upon it lay about a dozen books and a magnifying glass on top of a folded map; presumably of the Ordnance issue on mountain and coastal areas, but perhaps not; to the side, a brass compass and also a pair of field glasses. Beside the fire, on black iron hooks, were three pots and a pan. The pots were heavy cast iron, or appeared to be so, and the flattish pan was undoubtedly copper, or perhaps some alloy. It looked like an omelette pan and foreign…

Right beside my chair, for the time being, a long brass toasting fork lay angled to the fire; an old-fashioned and respected conductor of deep thought I had observed before here. There was no sign of breakfast except for a wheaten loaf, quite untouched in a small metal bin, and also a small flat wooden box, opened and containing about six or seven tins of nutritious salted, olive oiled and shiny Norwegian sardines.

On a small mantelshelf, there were only two Christmas cards and two empty envelopes, also some string and wax from a brown paper parcel. Beside the brown paper was a crystal plate, some decorative pine cones and a cake, quite small, with spiral white cream decorations amid chocolate. It looked expensive and had one candle, which looked as if it belonged on a long, far away and almost forgotten Christmas tree. On the mantel, too, was a copper eagle.

On the floor, beside the mantel, were a pair of faded white buckskin boots with a blue stamp, blurred by humidity; on each ankle, it said 'Changi 43'.

In one corner of the room was a Mauser sporting rifle with a powerful but somewhat old-fashioned telescopic sight. Beside it, a shoulder-high staff fashioned from a tree root, a tweed hat sat jauntily on the unusually long barrel of the rifle. They looked more like sentimental items, rather than for practical use. It was impossible for me to tell, although I had handled some rifles before, this one was quite different; it somehow had an air of futility about it.

Outside the cottage, the wind from the Atlantic was howling and blowing strongly across the edge of the mountains, but was deflected on the coastal side by a low dry stone wall curved around the cottage end.

The deep roar of the wind, however, was magically dampened by the wall into a low moan and then a sigh as it swept around the cottage and off to the eastern sea. The North Sea! The total effect of the curved wall was both to stop and quieten the wind blast and to deflect the snow in a simple and practical manner, for man or beast.

All such a different place than just two hours ago. No cottage, that, but a house, a home, and a fortress of seasonal happiness, or so it seemed then.

It was a few days after Christmas in North West Scotland. In mid-century Argyle. A meeting was to take place.

'I want you to meet someone this morning,' said our winter host, not addressing me.

'We will drive up the coast to see him,' he said, as he placed a large silver plate on the sideboard. On the platter was a mountain of 'scrambled eggs worcester', besieged by thick slices of ham and bacon with both round and link sausage, almost hiding some large pieces of fried tomato. The server was covered, too, with pieces of fresh green parsley and already black peppered bread sauce.

The silver platter was almost too interesting to eat, as it lay next to a similar platter of cold roast hill venison and beef with redcurrant jelly and a decorative set of mint leaves around a serving of mango chutney. Centerpieces for a robust breakfast after a stormy night in the house on the hillside above the town. All overlooking the Firth of Lorne and out into the cold Atlantic across to the islands of Mull and Iona.

This room was also warm, but from a large coal fire watching on a hearth of firebrick. It, too, spilled light and warmth into all corners of the room. There was a Christmas tree, too, in the bay window with the island background, and blushing evidence of this Christmas past everywhere. Outside and close by, the bells were still ringing as they had done all night, now dampened by the snow. Vespers and prayers, perhaps; sore, from cold cots, Carmelite ladies signaling devotion; lest we forget them or they us, as Christmas goes by again.

'The day just seems to go better after a good breakfast,' said our winter host, and not expecting an answer, pulling on his heavy double-breasted tweed overcoat and turned his royal blue woolen scarf around his neck, a small silver lion *couchant* guarding the tassels.

'He has a phone now, he keeps it under his bed. He is expecting us, soon.'

'Is this where he lives' the passenger asked, after a silent drive up the coast to the north. 'Yes, this is were he lives. All year round; he says it's all he needs.'

'Come in, come away in,' said the tallish figure, now stooping as he came through the door. He must have been watching for us. Wrapped in oiled wool and dark twill with a dash of green silk at the throat. He welcomed the three of us through the door of his cottage, taking our heavy winter coats in exchange for greetings, bowing and taking off his own open light border Cheviot jacket.

'You've picked the right time to visit, it will soon be the New Year and we still have very little snow. Some warmth for your insides then,' he said in a soft accent as he shepherded the others to the table and me to the comfortable fireside chair with a pat on the back, so I did not think that I had been forgotten.

From a bookshelf, two green bottles appeared. Just amber whisky from the triangular bottle into three glasses and, not often seen, good ginger wine for me, in a Jacobean crystal glass, from the other.

As they settled at the table, the atmosphere, without notice, changed entirely, as I watched and listened as best I could from my place by the fire, sweeping the place with my eyes. All three dropped into monotones as they raised their glasses. I did see a tear in one eye as our winter host proposed, 'The company'. Then all three repeated 'The good company,' in unison; one used the French *Campagnie,* it was quite clear, too, and curious.

I did not then exist and I really could not hear what they were saying, although they were only twelve feet away; a low roar from the bottom of the fire and wind in the chimney almost pushed away their conversation to the darkened end of the cottage to be lost. However, I noticed that when two of them stopped speaking, after a question was asked and one spoke with the answer I could hear something of what was said; but over about half an hour I still had no idea what the visit really was about. At this time of the year, three serious, ruby-like faces, reflecting the peat fire, around the table and no laughter was hard to explain, especially to me. Early on in the conversation I heard the word 'minesweepers'; I heard it twice, so I was not mistaken on that. I also heard the word 'hobbee' or 'obee'. There were no introductions when we arrived, so this may have been his name. I don't know and I wasn't going to ask, ever!

Just before we left, the conversation did flare up a bit as from surprise to an answered question. The man had said something like 'winter tour'. The other two looked at him and each other and repeated what they heard with a question mark and puzzlement in their faces.

Our winter host said, rather anxiously, 'What code? Do you know?'

The man replied in the manner of the French, *'Troisième!* Up the stone steps. Second floor.'

'It cannot be, they are friends of ours. He is RN too!' said the passenger.

As we drove down the winding track, sheltered by low pines, the man in the passenger seat said, 'I don't believe it! Even if I'd seen it for myself! Him living there, I mean. He is the highest paid man in our organization. How does he do it?'

'Oh, it's really quite simple,' said our winter host. 'Everybody, just everybody, trusts him!'

'Not at all like the fellow on the eastern coast,' said the passenger. 'He was the most decorated man in the force and nobody knew much about him either. Couldn't hit a golf ball though; a terrible slice, no control whatsoever.'

'Oh, I'm not surprised at that!' said the winter host. 'But back to business. Where does Shellenberg stay these days?'

'Always the same place,' said the passenger. 'In the Old Town; Grays Wynd. Steep and slippery in the rain and all cobbled! Second floor above the cross. That's the house with the attic and skylight overlooking the entire town and out to the bridge and the naval dockyard. He muses that everyone who has ever served in the Royal Navy in the last century has passed within fifty feet of his armchair! It's probably true, too, I saw it!'

'Well, you'd better tell him what we just heard,' said our winter host. 'Also, *troisième* is on the second floor too! He'll need a fur coat for that place at this time of the year, and all kinds of courage, and some!'

'Better him than me,' said the passenger. 'Do you think that he can pull it off? It's a single shot assignment, you know! No second chance there!'

Piece of cake, I thought, half asleep already in the backseat of the Mark Four Jaguar.

CPSIA information can be obtained
at www.ICGtesting.com
Printed in the USA
LVOW11*2153240917

549912LV00004B/7/P